B.D. Pedersen

DIMENSION '53'

Edited by
June Pedersen

ISBN: 978-0692212783
0692212787

Prologue

Imagine living in the state of Kansas and getting up one wonderful morning, having breakfast and then taking your cup of coffee out onto the back porch. Then imagine standing there taking in the beauty of the wide-open spaces around you and right in the middle of the view you see a stranger standing in a plowed field across the road from your driveway.

Now, what's so odd about that? Well, I guess nothing unless you noticed the man was well dressed and absolutely did not fit in, especially where he was standing. To make matters worse, as you focus on him, he up and disappears, just like that. Yes, you heard me right. He plain disappeared. First, he was there and then he was not there. How else can

I say it?

What I was to find out shortly was he would be back and each time he came back the mystery would get much more involved. Where did he come from? What was he doing? Why was he coming to the field across from my farmhouse? Who was he?

The really terrifying thing about it, he appeared and would continue to appear because of me, he was targeting me in particular. What I would learn over the next nine to twelve weeks and it was going to change my life, leaving me not knowing reality from fantasy.

What started out as a mystery would become a revelation that would shock my basic fundamental concept of reality. I would learn there is more to this universe than I had ever thought of or really wanted to know.

On that bright sunny morning I was a man happy with my own lifestyle and wanting to see it continue as it always had. When he came into my life it left me with a feeling of vulnerability and a nagging fear it would never end.

Have I pricked your curiosity yet? If I have then what you're about to witness may leave you a little dumbfounded. Don't worry, it won't bother you for long. You won't have time to be bothered. You'll be spending your time trying to determine if what you just witnessed was fact or fiction, whether it was a threat to you, or if the events just involved me.

Come on now, you're a grown person. Open your mind and let it take in the reality of what has happened around this small farm house in the middle of the country and away from most of the nation's population. The most serious threat to the welfare and freedom of this nation was faced and taken down, for the time being that is.

I find I must tell you, all of you, what happened. The government will deny anything and everything I say, but they do that with everything anyway. All I can do is tell things like they happened and you will have to decide what the truth is and what is not. If nothing else, I want you to realize these things can and do happen and unless you're prepared and willing to accept that necessity, we are lost as a nation, for that matter as a world.

How the government could even begin to explain away the solid concrete monolith that eventually ended up sitting on the land across from my home will, in itself, be most interesting.

Please, read on with an open mind and give yourself the opportunity of learning something that can change everything you thought you knew and probably much more about those things you did not know. In the end it all may be for the better, for you and for me.

Chapter One

A HISTORY LESSON

World War Two had been going on for about four and a half years when the final battle in Europe took place. Japan would continue to fight into September of 1945 while Germany surrendered on May 7, 1945.

The major issue in the surrender of Germany was the finding of Adolph Hitler and bringing him to justice. The Russian army had been given the task of invading Berlin and ending the war with Germany. What the allies didn't know was Hitler and his staff had made plans in regards to their escape from the invading Russian military, and subsequent world courts that would be following the war. In doing that, making good their escape, they would become a major threat to the world some sixty-seven years later.

In the final hours of Berlin, the planned moves by the leaders of the German government called for them to assemble in the north of Germany around where the V2 rockets had been developed, produced and launched from. Besides the development of the V2 and other military advanced weaponry the Germans had been playing with a new machine and concept, notably "Time and Dimension Travel."

As the Russian army took control of Berlin and located the numerous governmental leaders they were after, they found many of them dead by suicide. At least that was what they assumed had happened.

The bodies of Hitler and his new wife Eva were found outside their bunker. They had been burned and there was little evidence to prove it was in fact Hitler. The greatest mystery of all was the fact they were unable to clearly and totally ensure the bodies found were in fact those of Hitler and his Command Staff.

Nor could they prove they, the command staff and Hitler, had not committed suicide but had actually disappeared, their location unknown at the time. There was a lot of speculation that Hitler had in fact escaped, and the body found was a double and not Hitler's. The speculation increased over the years and the answers never were really made clear as to whether the body found was in fact his.

But what would happen if he had not committed suicide, and in fact he and his associates had switched a double for him, and that double paid the ultimate price and was killed and then burned so as to totally void any attempt to actually identify the body that was found.

And to carry this speculation just a little further, what if the bodies of the other command staff of Hitler's were also doubles who had been killed, to be found by the allies as they invaded the country.

What if the German scientists actually did develop a dimension machine? What if it was used that week in May of 1945 to move Hitler and his main contingent of staff personnel to another dimension in another universe, or some other place in this universe? What if he and his bunch had actually escaped the judgment of the world and would, in time, become an even greater threat than they had been during the war?

So many of the higher-ranking people of the German government dropped out of sight at the time, some were found and those were tried. Some were executed and others managed to still commit suicide. But what if they were all committed Nazi doubles and they had carried out their duties to the Furor and the greater plan of the German Nazi Government.

During the year 1944 the German scientists were working on a number of strange and unbelievable weapons. They were working hard to perfect a nuclear bomb, but it would prove to be unattainable for them. They worked hard on a saucer type aircraft, but it too failed as so many other concepts had.

However, found in the region of their most advanced weapons research was a strange concrete and steel framed structure, known as the 'Henge', which had no apparent purpose whatsoever. As you stood there and looked at the thing it became apparent it was a structure designed to hold some massive machine. This machine became known as the 'The Bell' or 'Die Clocke' also referred to as 'The Nazi-Bell'.

It was this machine some speculate

about to this day; it was a real time machine and Hitler and his cohorts made their escape by the means of a time or interdimensional machine. Now, I'm not saying this was the truth, all I'm saying is it was a theory and one that could well be true, yet there is no way of proving it.

So, let's assume it is true and 'The Bell' and the 'Henge' structures were in fact real and this monster of a man did make his escape into the future or some other dimension. What could we then expect of them here in our own time and our own place?

I had not really thought about World War II and all the things that came with it, but at my age one was really not expected to. After all the Second World War was old history now and the past really was of no concern to those of us in this day and age. I would eventually realize there was something to be concerned about from that time, those places, the madness, which would land square in front of me, leaving no escape route of denial.

Never in my wildest dreams or nightmares would I come to the understanding we as a nation, a world, a dimension, needed to be concerned about any threat from another dimension or time.

I am a simple person. I grew up in a quiet part of Kansas just a few hundred feet away from the geographical center of the lower forty-eight states. I hadn't even concerned myself with anything about the old war. It just wasn't high on my interest list.

Yes, I've seen just about every war movie out there is and I too have my favorites in this category. But, the aspects of war simply do not have a high level of priority in my life. In fact, I abhor even the idea of war regardless of the rational used to justify it. In this day and age men need to use their minds and good sense to deal with their differences and not do it through the specter of war.

However, I am interested in the scientific probability of space and all the physical properties which comes with that line of study. I watch with great interest the growth of our space exploration, though I frankly am not a hands-on scientific type person.

What the hell is all this rambling about anyway? I'm sitting here babbling like a lost kid and really don't have the slightest idea as to what I'm really wanting to say. I guess I'm trying to figure a way to start telling you my story, but I'm having one heck of a time getting things organized. I mean where do I really start and what do I need to say to get your attention as to what we, as a world, are facing.

What you need to know is that what took place sixty-four some years ago is important today, in fact it's even more important now than it was fifty, sixty or seventy years ago. What took place within the German war machine during the final days of World War two were coming back to kill us now and we had better get our heads together and learn to deal with it.

I know and I have seen it and I am telling you right now, pay attention and get your heads out of your butts. The government will deny everything I am telling you and may even take action against me. But if they do, then there is likely to be something to what I am saying and it will shine a greater light on what I'm trying to tell you.

Look, don't sit there and roll your eyes, let me lay it out for you and then you be the judge as to whether I have something that needs to be looked at in depth, and maybe the people need to know there is a real issue here and our government had better start getting their act together and working up a future defense against what is there on the other side.

And the monolith, it's standing there right now as big as a three-story building and for no apparent reason or purpose. Why would someone pour that much concrete in one area and not have a specific reason? So, it's time for me to tell you how it got there and what it is actually there for. The fact is, there are ten of these monoliths situated across the nation and world and they are all there for the same reason.

Now before I begin, I need to say one more thing and please do not let this interfere with your willingness to hear me out. I am not an expert in the art of war or in the development of technology or the scientific understanding of dimensions. I am a writer and nothing more, a writer who has witnessed something and took the steps to bring the government into the situation because it was way outside my ability to deal with it.

If you don't trust our government then you're going to question my action critically and that may cause you to resist hearing me out but I ask you to be patient. I would suggest you take the time to calm yourself and let the facts settle in before you judge. When I'm done you can judge as you, please.

Chapter Two

TODD MEETS TODD

If I were to tell you, you were living multiple existences, what would you think? You would probably think I was crazy or something akin to that. But, I'm here to tell you, you do exist in more than one place at the same time. In fact, there are probably thousands of you living and carrying on varied lives all at the same time and in the same place.

Yes, I said, in the same place. The only difference is each separate place is in a different dimension. You know, one of those places that run parallel with this dimension, your reality exits in at this moment.

What if I were to tell you there were in

fact thousands of other dimensions, all existing right next to one another parallel to each other, and separated by just a simple shift in time and space. Men far more intelligent than I am have developed theories predicting the presence of these dimensions. They use terms like Quantum Mechanics, String Theory and M-Theory or Membranes. All say there are dimensions besides the one we live in.

I'm not a scientist, I'm just a guy who, by simple accident, discovered the many dimensions that are there, existing along with us in our own dimension. My name is Todd Hancock. I live in the outskirts of Lebanon, Kansas, about one and three quarters of a mile northwest of Lebanon. My home is on State Route 191 and is just six hundred eighty-five feet east of the center of the lower forty-eight states.

How I ended up there is nothing big, I was born there and lived my whole life there, well the thirty-three years of my life so far. My parents farmed in this area and as a child I did what all farm kids did. When I was old enough, I had chores and in time worked as a farm hand. During that time, I attended school and eventually graduated from Smith Center

High School just to the west of where I lived.

I stayed in the area working with my dad and when he passed on, I took over the operation of the farm. After mom passed on, I decided to sell the farm land and retain and live in the home which I inherited from my parents. I really was not a farmer, and had no desire to be one. So, what does one do for a living in this area that is not a part of the farming community, the economic and job foundation for this part of Kansas?

Well, I started writing. My parents left me rather well off and so I really did not have to work, as long as I lived fairly frugally and within my means. With the advent of computers and then the internet one had the ability to travel anywhere and research anything and from that develop any number of topics to write about. So, I became interested in the little-known things of this world. I found this to be fairly interesting and somewhat in demand.

Now, what has that got to do with dimensions and little-known things about the world? Well really nothing. That's right nothing. I have never had any interest in science or dimensions in particular. I guess you could say it just happened. Yes, I think that is the right description, it just happened.

The next question that comes to mind is why did it happen? And, my friends I will have to say, I have not the slightest idea. I couldn't even begin to give you a logical and believable reason as to how and why it happened, it just did. That's it, it just did.

The fact is I didn't even know it when it first happened. I mean I was standing in my backyard looking out toward the marker for the center of the country. In fact, I wasn't thinking of anything, know what I mean. I had my morning cup of coffee and had stepped outside that wonderful early August morning and there I was.

Like so many things that happen in life there were no warnings or indications something was about to take place. Millions of people throughout history have experienced the same thing. They wake up one morning and go about their daily business when it happens. It lands on them, no warning, no signs of it coming. Like a meteor falling out of the sky and landing on you.

From my point of view there is absolutely no reason why this event should happen to me. Why did providence choose me in the first place? Was it because of where I lived? Or, maybe it was the fact I was picked lottery style and here I am? I mean, give me a break, why me?

So, I got up that morning and did my usual thing and then headed to the kitchen for some breakfast. I'm one who believes in a good breakfast to start the day. It took me around forty-five minutes to fix and eat it and then I took my coffee and headed outside. It was a nothing special day and I expected nothing special. And, so when I stepped out the back door, I had my second awakening for the day.

There he was, I mean, no that's not want I want to say. Wait, yes, there he was standing there. A man! Yes, just a man, nothing special about him except he was standing in the field across from my house watching me or my house. Something like that just does not appear out of nowhere. I mean, he was not dressed like me or anyone else I knew. He could have been a transient, except his dress yelled wealth and social position. Come on now, no person just pops up, but this one did.

All I did was stand there. Dimensions never even entered my mind. He was a well dressed and stately man and he had no business being there. What the hell was I to think? I don't know how long I stood there looking at him. I mean, what would you do? After about five minutes or however the hell long it was, he suddenly went away. I mean, he disappeared, he was gone, hell I don't know what I mean.

He left. He was there and then he left. The only thing he could have been was a mirage. That was it, he was a mirage. But he looked so real. No, he was a mirage and I left it at that.

The next day I was at the computer so I decided to do some research on mirages. What I found caused me to determine what I had seen was not a mirage. A mirage is an optical phenomenon in which a view of an object some distance away may be seen and can be photographed.

Strange, that didn't come close to describing what I had seen the day before. No, he had to be a mirage, what else could he have been, the real thing? That was not possible because he wasn't out there now and when I looked at the ground over there it did not look like anything had been sitting on it. It was plowed ground and nothing else.

Later on, that day I happened to be in

Lebanon for a short meeting at city hall. While there I saw a couple of friends who live and farm out in my area, about three miles from my place. I went over to Fred.

As seldom as you see people you know you don't pass up a chance to stop and talk to one another, "Fred how are things going over your way?"

He looked up and when he saw me, he walked over to me, "Hi Todd. We're doing well. Harvest is getting underway and it all looks great."

I knew I had to ask him if he had seen any strangers around our area in the past day or two. "Hey Fred did you see anything odd over along the 191 yesterday? It would have been in the field across from my driveway."

He stood there running his hands through his hair. "Why no I can't say I did. What time would it have been?"

"Around eight in the morning, I was in my backyard and saw something over in the field across the 191 from my house."

He stood there and shook his head. "No, I can't say I did. What did you see?"

That was the question I was waiting for and I was not sure just how I was going to answer it. "Not sure Fred. It looked like a stranger at least he was to me. Never saw him before, but I'm sure it was probably my imagination. What would a stranger be doing standing in an open field? He didn't even have a car." I wasn't going to tell him I saw him disappear though.

He looked to his wife and asked her and she said no. Then he turned back to me, "A stranger? No, haven't seen any strangers in this area for a long time."

Odd, I would think if any strangers were in the area someone else would have seen them. People don't just walk around the area without being noticed. "Yes, that's what I thought. Must have been a mirage or something like that. Thanks Fred."

Fred nodded and shrugged his shoulders. "Any time Todd. How's everything else going?"

That's how it is around farm country. You never stop and talk without asking about the well being of the other. "Just fine, been thinking about taking a trip out west next month. I would like to get away for a few days before winter sets in. How are you and the family doing?"

He smiled and nodded. "Now that sounds great. Hey, you see that mirage thing again give me a call so I can take a look. And, the Family, we're doing great, thanks."

I told myself, like I'll do that first thing, "That I'll do Fred. Thanks again. Bye."

Fred waved, turned and walked off saying over his shoulder. "Take it easy Todd, see ya."

Really now, if there had been a man standing out there at the center of the USA, someone else would have seen him. I must have seen a mirage or was I day dreaming. Strange I had never had this happen before. So, I marked it up as an oddity and decided to let it go, little did I know it was not going to, no not by a far sight.

It must have been three weeks later. I was sitting in my den working on an article for a sports magazine when I happened to look up and out the window. There he was, the same man and this time he was standing beside what looked like a car, but was clearly not one. The sun was washing over him and reflecting off the window of the vehicle. What the hell, twice.

I got up and went outside and stood there looking at him. He was standing there looking at me. Now for a mirage, this was one hell of a realistic one. Just then he waved at me. I looked again and he waved again. I turned and looked around and then back at the guy and he pointed at me and then waved again.

I turned and ran into the house and got my binoculars and ran back outside. I got them to my eyes and focused in on the man. I froze. There he was looking at me and smiling. So, why should that make me freeze? Maybe because the man I was looking at was me. Yeah, that's right, me.

I stood there watching him and then he held a sign up. I focused the binoculars again and looked at the sign. It read, "Hi Todd, nice to meet you." I dropped the binoculars and stood there.

Camera? Camera? Where the hell is that camera anyway? I ran back into the house and through the house looking for it and finally found it on my desk under some papers. I grabbed it and ran back outside and as I brought it up, he and his car flashed away.

All I could do was stand there. Was I crazy? Did I actually see what I thought I saw? Could it possibly have been me over there in the field? He signaled me by name, so that must mean something. One thing was for sure, this was not a mirage. And, if it was not a mirage, then what the heck was it. Now I was really confused and questioning everything I had seen.

I consider myself a fairly rational man. I mean it takes a lot to get me going, but this thing just floored me. For a minute there I felt like I was going to pass out. I mean my head went light and I broke out into a cold sweat. This was crazy. Twice now, I have seen it, him, twice and it was the same both times.

Now look, let me think this out. He looked like me and that could have been a car of some kind he was standing by. It was sleek and gold colored. I think I remember the car was a two door, or maybe it was a four door, and was parked parallel to the 191 road. No, it was the real thing.

Yet this thing did not feel right. Why would someone show up across from my home and not try to make a direct one on one contact? Instead, he holds up a handmade sign and shows it to me, it simply does not make since. "Hi Todd nice to meet you." what kind of a greeting or first contact was that anyway?

As I walked back into the house, I decided if this thing happened again, I was going to be ready for it. I set the binoculars and camera on the counter top by the back door so they would be ready the next time, if there was a next time. Something deep down inside told me there would be a next time. This thing was not over yet, not by a long shot.

My mind was ablaze with thoughts and considerations. Nothing I came up with seemed to offer any kind of a realistic answer to what was going on. It defied all logic and understanding. No, there was a logical reason for these events and I needed to sit down and skull it out.

I grabbed a writing pad and started writing down everything I had seen. I started with date, day and time. I recorded the weather conditions and any other normal and natural aspect of any given day this time of the year. Had there been any odd atmospheric conditions that had been evident on the first day I saw him and this day?

What were my physical conditions at the time of the first happening and then today? I had gotten plenty of sleep the nights before and I feel great now, as I did the first time it happened. I was not taking any medicines that could cause me to hallucinate. Last, but not least, I had not been fantasizing. I'm a fairly rational man and I don't go around day dreaming about anything let alone a man popping in and out of nowhere.

As I was writing, it dawned on me things like this do not happen. I can see a onetime event if I were sick or whatever, but not twice and if twice then it would probably happen again.

As I looked at my notes, I realized the time period between this happening and the first one was exactly three weeks. It was three weeks to the day and hour. If I had kept good records of each event they would have probably been to the exact minute as well.

If I was right, then it would mean in three weeks to the day, hour, and minute he would return to that exact same place and probably in the same vehicle. I wrote a large note and taped it to my computer and then sat back looking at it. I would be ready in three weeks and seeing this thing through.

Still my mind was trying to rationalize this whole thing. I'm sorry, I can't help it. I'm a rational man and my mind must find a reason, a rational reason for what I saw and I still felt it was something physical.

My next concern was the reason for this being showing up here and how he did it. The 191 is a well used road in this area and normally when a vehicle comes along you can hear it. It's not that the level of traffic is so heavy or there's the continuous sound of traffic noise coming from the road. However, when I'm anywhere near the back of the house I will hear cars and trucks as they come by. I heard no traffic noise either of those two mornings.

In addition, there were no signs of a vehicle pulling into the field. No tire marks or disturbed ground. I did find where something had been sitting on the ground, but there is no trail from the road to that position. Odd, there was no way a vehicle could get to that spot without leaving a trail of some kind, but it did.

Why the three-week period between visits? In just two visits I could not say a three-week period was normal, but the fact is he did not come back until exactly three weeks after the first visit which seems to say there will be a three-week period between the second and third visit as well. We will see about that, but this next time I will be ready and I will see him come in.

I had considered calling on a couple of writer friends of mine and getting their opinions but decided I would be better off not doing that. How could I contact others and tell them this story and still have them consider me a rational man? No, for the time being I would leave anyone else out of this. If after the next appearance, if there is one, I can consider bringing someone else in on this event. In a way I was feeling a sense of excitement and anticipation and was clearly eager to see if I was right about the time schedule. Anyway, we will see, in three weeks.

Three weeks caused me to sit back and review what I had seen in relationship to a schedule that was indicated. Clearly this person, this other me, did not drive into that spot and parked those two times.

The first time I didn't see the car and the second time it was there. That was a fair-sized car and I would have seen it when it parked across the road from my driveway. No, it had not been there and the second time it was. What did that mean?

It could possibly mean a progressive schedule. Whoever, was involved in this thing, was doing it in a controlled manner and on a schedule. How could I say that? Well, when I looked at the time between the two visits, I find a definite period of time and I found when he came the second time it was right on the money with the first time. No, he was keeping a schedule which meant there was something more behind it. He was not a guy running around from place to place for the hell of it. There was planning and support behind him.

If this were true then it meant there was a specific reason for his being here at this place and at this time. In addition, he looked like me and I have a feeling he is me. He knew my name and had it on a sign he held up. The fact he took the time to write the sign and bring it with him means he expected to find me here and he planned on making contact with me.

By now I was beginning to feel a little scared. This was not a happenstance thing. It was planned and premeditated on his part and those who were behind him. Something big was coming out of this and I needed to dig into it a little deeper. I needed to think hard on both meetings. What did I actually see each time?

It became a situation where I had to gain control of myself and settle into a recall of the first event and clearly and logically layout everything that happened during the event. There are things within an event which will be important and I was sure would give me vital information on the second event.

When I first saw him standing there my reaction was twofold. What was a stranger doing standing in the field? And second, accepting the fact he was there. What was his purpose? I recalled I had considered him to be a mirage, a miracle of nature that carries with it a degree of mystery and beauty that has touched mankind for as long as there has been time. I needed to deal with that issue sometime soon.

The next time would bring this issue in to direct contrast and cause me to accept the truth of the moment and the fact this other me was actually real and was taking a progressive means of making a one-on-one contact with me. It was going to happen and I needed to be prepared for it. I had a strong feeling when I learned the truth of what was happening, it would be stranger than anything I had come up with so far.

Damn, I was in the process of meeting myself and I had not the slightest idea as to what I should prepare for or how I should be planning this thing. Obviously, he had been and was working through a plan and I was one of his targets in his plan. The question was what was the purpose of his targeting me? That left me not just uneasy, but almost sick.

When I reviewed the second coming it was obvious a major change had taken place with the presence of the car, well what I thought was a car. If it had been there during the first meeting, I had not seen it, so this meant it must have been there but not visible to me at the time. In the second meeting the machine was clearly there.

I managed to get pictures of this meeting and saw the sign he had shown to me. The time of the meeting was exactly three weeks to the hour from the first appearance. I noted the fact he told me he would be back in three weeks, so I knew the exact time and place of the next meeting and I needed to be prepared.

How the hell do you prepare for a meeting with yourself? Second, how do you prepare for a meeting with someone who just pops in and out of existence? Those are issues you simply can't prepare for. All you can do is be there and be ready to react to whatever takes place. Right now, I was somewhat scared, but I also was not concerned about any physical assault. No, the fear thing was the oddity in the manner in which this thing was happening. It was the unknown this situation was loaded with I feared above all else.

Three weeks, that was the target and it would become the focal point for all my actions from here until then, if he returned. I was almost looking forward to it.

Chapter Three

MIRAGE VS DIMENSIONS

It hadn't dawned on me yet a dimension issue may be involved here. My mind was stuck on the mirage thing. The fact of the matter was I had no concept of dimensions at all. Yes, I knew about dimensions as far as measurements are concerned or any other application when it came to size or area. But, dimensions in respect to other worlds or universes hadn't even touched me, I didn't have a clue.

It was three weeks later, about the middle of August, I was pulling into the driveway and as I came around the corner of the house heading for the garage, I saw the other me and the car again. Damn I had been so busy working for this moment I actually forgot it. I had forgotten to check my computer and see the note on it. It was plain dumb luck I had returned home at that moment. When I checked my watch, I was but seconds late, so he had not been waiting. I stopped the car and jumped out and ran to the back door and grabbed the camera.

This time I got the picture. In fact, I kept taking pictures and then set the camera to video and ran video as long as I could. As I finished with the camera, I put the binoculars to my eyes and focused in on this new me. This time I was studying me more than just looking at me. He appeared to be dressed the same as he had been before. But even more important I was not sure this other being was me.

I stood there looking across at me and then he picked up a sign and showed it to me, it read, "Todd, I'm from a parallel dimension. I'll be back in three weeks and then I will come over to meet you."

Hey, why not come over now? What's all this beating around the bush anyway? If you want to talk to me then come on over now and we'll talk.

That was it. He and the car then flashed

off again. I stood there and tried to understand what I had read and seen. It then registered to me he had gotten back into the machine before it flashed off. I had failed to write that down before and when I considered it, which is what he had done the time before. The first time there had been no machine present, that I saw anyway. Yet I remember him reaching out and bending over and getting into something. How could I miss that, he got into something I could not see?

Not only had he gotten into an invisible something but as he opened the door or whatever he opened I could see into the thing and then watched as he got in and then closed the opening.

Oh, this was getting good and he was feeding me information a bit at a time like he was leading me along to some point or some situation in which I would become a major participant in whatever it was he was working on.

He said he was from a parallel dimension. What was that? He was coming back in three weeks to actually meet me. No, that's not possible. What the hell is a parallel dimension? Three weeks, why that period of time? I was now fairly sure the three-week thing was a normal or standard schedule.

As I thought about it, the other sightings had been in three-week intervals, just as I had put on the note pad and had placed on my computer to remind me of today, lot of good that did.

I went back into the house and to my computer and did a search on dimensions and about one hundred nineteen million sites came up. For the next three weeks I was going to be learning everything I could about dimensions and their reality or fantasy. In three weeks, I wanted to have some questions ready for this guy, whoever he was, and I wanted some answers some meaning to what was going on.

If there were other dimensions, what would or could that mean to us here in this one? Up till now I had no idea as to whether other dimensions actually existed. I had seen and read the usual stuff on dimensions and the reasoning the scientists give for them, but no real experience or self belief in these things had been a part of me. No, dimensions were still a mystery to me and I needed to learn a whole lot about them and in a short time.

If they did actually exist, they did not have any effect on me or this world or dimension of ours that I knew of. At least that's what I thought until now. My first problem was I was having a hard time accepting the idea of another world or universe or whatever being right along side of me, but on a different plain.

There was no way something like this could cause any kind of an issue for us here in this world or time or place. No, there had to be something else going on here. I could believe an alien from another planet somewhere else in the Galaxy was doing this, and I could be meeting a being who has taken my physical appearance and is now trying to contact me.

But what if it was true? He was from another dimension, then what? I have no idea. So what? It would mean nothing. He will come and visit and then leave and that would be it. Probably some guy playing with a hobby and he managed to punch through the barrier between our two dimensions and now he's playing with it. But who would want to play with the barriers between dimensions? Wouldn't that be dangerous or something? I don't know, but it's something to think about.

All right, I still need to learn a little about dimensions so I can ask some reasonably intelligent question concerning what he was up to and doing. Who knows, he may be the first contact in an invasion of our dimension and its takeover.

All right, what should I ask him? Let's see, I could ask him if he is me. Dumb, of course he is me, he looks just like me. Well then, I could ask him what his dimension looks like. That's a little bit better and is relevant to my life here and its relationship to his. How about, "Is what you're doing dangerous to our two dimensions?" Now I'm clearly getting a little more involved. Yes, I like that one.

Let's see, I have three weeks to get a true list of questions put together and it means I need to learn a lot more about dimensions and what they are and where they are. The problem is with the little bit of research I had already done left me even more confused than I was when I started.

Why the car or whatever? Now that was odd. Surely there must be a reason for it. I mean he was bringing a car across the line and that must take a huge amount of power and energy. Why not a motorcycle or something small and simple? Well, whatever, the fact is, I need to know more about what is coming than I do now.

Could it be I was still seeing a mirage and it was not a dimensional traveler after all? Granted it would be a one in a million mirage, but that seems to be more logical than a dimensional traveler of some kind. Really, what is a mirage?

When I first looked the information up on the internet, what came out of the research was rather complex and extensive. But, the basic description of a mirage dealt with the bending or refraction of light.

Basically, when the atmospheric conditions are right, the light coming toward you can be bent and in doing that it acts more like a lens and this lens lets you see an object even if it is over the horizon. As I said before, the light is bent to produce a displaced image of a distant object.

The significant thing about this is the object can also be something that is moving. It does not have to be a stationary object. However, as you approach the object or mirage, it continues to stay a distance from you until you pass through the environment producing the image or until you reach the actual object you're seeing.

In other words, the object never really comes into close proximity to you. Second, it never really appears to be a solid object. It has a semitransparent appearance. If a solid object were to pass through it nothing would waver or change, the object would move along in the mirage until it was clear of it.

There are two types of mirages one being a superior and the other an inferior mirage. If you are looking at a superior mirage you will actually see there is a line of sky under it that separates the mirage from the ground or terrain ahead of you. An inferior mirage will appear as a lake or water on the roadway ahead of you or on any flat surface you are facing.

This brings one other issue up and its distance. A mirage is always off and away from you. If it is an inferior mirage it appears to be water on the road, or a lake on a flat section of land ahead of you. You never drive into the road mirage or step into the land mirage. It will always be down the road from you or just out ahead of you as long as the atmospheric conditions remain in effect.

A superior mirage will always sit off in the distance and you will never be able to gain any closer relationship with it. Also, it is above the horizon and you can see a strip of sky between it and the ground it is situated over. Again, it will remain as long as the conditions don't change and once, they do change, they fade out of view.

No, what I was seeing from my back yard those prior two times and this time was not a mirage. I wish it actually was, because if it's not then it can only be one other thing and that's a dimensional shift or whatever. There is nothing else I can find or determine that would put a person and a car sitting in a field across the road from my home without having been driven there.

So, what is a dimension? That my friend is a good question, and I don't have the slightest idea, well maybe I should say, I can't even begin to grasp an understanding as to what a dimension is.

Now I do know about the first three dimensions. You know height, width, and depth. We all see them every moment of every day we're awake. You look at an object and it has a depth and a width and a height. Everything we see in this world has those three elements.

But then there comes the fourth dimension and this is where I start to lose it. What the hell is a fourth dimension? Well, I managed to do some additional research and found the fourth dimension has been identified by numerous people and has been related to many different things.

One defined it as being one's consciousness. Upon death we, our consciousness, move into the fourth dimension, whatever the heck that meant. But I was able to learn with the advent of Einstein's Theory of Relativity, time is now seen as the fourth dimension.

So, what does this give me? Well, it tries to give me the physical properties of this universe. But not of a place that was not of this universe, a place that runs parallel to this universe, but was separated from it and was in itself another universe. Is this possible? If I am to believe what I have seen so far, then yes, it is possible.

The next question to comes to mind is, how many other universes can there be, or for that matter other dimensions? Have I got you confused yet? Believe me when I tell you I'm really confused. It's just a bunch of bull and I'm not sure if I have made any rational headway at all. I have finally come to the conclusion I can't grasp something I cannot see. With that I've decided to just wait until the other person, who appears to be me, comes back and then go from there. What else can I do?

I know. I can start preparing for the return of me and record it in its entirety. That's it. I'll set up a number of cameras and recorders so everything can be recorded for future review and study. That will be my job over these next three weeks, to prepare for his return.

Dimensions, axis, fourth, fifth, whatever, I had this odd feeling I was going to understand all of it before this was over. My only concern was would anyone believe me when I tell them?

I was beginning to feel like I was in a state of irrationality, a state of confusion where reality simply becomes fuzzy and out of focus. All I could do was sit there and let my mind run. Maybe if I took a nap I could wake up and all this would turn out to be a dream.

Well anyway, I knew a mirage was probably not the explanation for what I was experiencing. And, if we're not experiencing a mirage, then it had to be a dimensional thing and I would need to prepare myself for that reality.

But how the hell does one prepare for

another dimension, whatever it is? That was what was really bothering me. It wasn't the fact this guy was popping in and out of reality, it was the fact if he was from another dimension then what could or would the ramifications be?

As I sat there and let my imagination roll, I began to realize there could be all sorts of issues I should take into consideration. What about the actual coming together of two like beings from different dimensions? Would it result in an explosion or some other cataclysmic result?

Is it possible the other Todd could be carrying some virus we have never experienced in this dimension and he could transfer it to me and start an epidemic? That one could literally destroy the human race in this dimension.

The fact was, the more I thought about this whole thing the crazier it became. Finally, I decided I needed to just let it sit and wait out the three weeks. During this time, I would buy the video equipment I was thinking about and set things up for the coming event.

I also knew I needed to prepare myself for the eventual meeting I was apparently going to have with this person. In a way, I was excited about the prospects of having a one on one with this person. God knows what would or could come from this meeting.

As a writer I was thinking about all sorts of ideas and articles that could come from this meeting. For this reason alone, it was important I get all the documentation I could get on this meeting and everything and anything that comes from it. With something as complex as this situation was becoming, I couldn't trust my memory alone to capture everything and anything happening.

No, the video and still cameras were a must in this situation and I needed to get on with the project as soon as possible. It would take time to set them up and make sure everything was working properly.

In addition, I had decided I needed to place the cameras in places and in position where they were not readily seen. My visitor did not need to know I was recording everything. I would have my hand camera and when he sees it, he may or may not object. That we would deal with when the time came. But the presence of a camera would or could cover any concern about other cameras being around and in use.

Chapter Four

I'M COMING

I don't know. I've tried to understand the difference between a mirage and a dimension. I know what a mirage is and I know what I saw was not a mirage. But, dimensions? That's a totally different thing. It's just crazy. They, the scientists speak of axis and x, y, and z and it means little to me. I'm not a scientist and I'm not a great thinker. I simply saw something and I'm trying to understand it.

Was it really me standing in the field with those signs? It sure looked like me. Can a man just appear in an empty field? It just doesn't happen, yet it sure as hell did. No, I'm going to have to wait and see if he returns and if so, see what happens next. I can do nothing else, nothing more.

Two more weeks and it's killing me. So, I set to work building my security and observation system. I went out and purchased a dozen high resolutions color video cameras, along with exterior housings, cables, power systems, and lenses. I installed sound systems and mics everywhere I could think of. I even bought a second computer to control and monitor all the equipment. I was determined to record every possible part of his return and time here.

When I was done, and it took me eight days to do it, I had my entire property, the road and field across the road from me covered as well. I had put two cameras on the roof of the house aimed at the field where the man and car were last seen. Each camera was set at the opposite end of the house from one another so I would get a wide-angle view of the field.

Along with those two cameras I installed two infrared cameras so I could record the heat levels of any object in the field and be able to record what was happening during the night. I actually went across to the field and installed two cameras on the fence and set them up on photocell battery systems.

I then set cameras up on the porch of the house covering the driveway and garage area and the lawn between there and the road and of course the porch. Inside I installed a camera in each room with sound mics as well.

I installed four, two terabyte hard drive recorders, and attached them to the computer. The computer was set to oversee the trafficking of all video signals coming in from the cameras. The cameras on top of the house were on recorder one. The porch, driveway and garage cameras were on recorder two. The two field cameras were sent to recorder three and the remaining interior cameras went to recorder four.

Next, I set the computer to record on a twenty-four-hour basis and to recycle the hard drives every forty-eight hours which would clear the storage drives and start a new forty-eight-hour recording period. In this way I could simply hit a hot key to extend or by pass the recycle if I needed to. Once the hot key was hit the system would record continuously until the hard drives were full. Each drive would record from six hundred seventy-five to seven hundred hours of video. This gave me ample amounts of video storage.

Once everything was set up, I then installed a motion activation system so when the "me" appeared, his appearance would activate the sensors and they in turn would start the recording. I went over the design and install process a number of times till I felt I was ready for this event when and if it happened.

How should one react or act when he meets himself? Do I just act like he was anyone and shake his hand or do I try to form an understanding between the two of us? Hell, I don't even know what I'm saying. I don't know what to say or do, so I'll just play it by ear when and if he comes.

Then the thought hit me. When two beings from different dimensions meet and touch, what happens? Would it be like matter and anti-matter, they annihilate each other? That's a comforting thought. Yeah, I had thought of it before, but as it came closer it became more ominous. So maybe I better stand back or away from him at first until I'm sure we won't destroy the world or something.

Another thing, will we be identical? I mean everything about us, our fingerprints, blood makeup, physical build, and so on, would it all be the same? Would our thoughts be the same once we're together? Does he live on a farm in the middle of Kansas someplace? Is there a Kansas there? Where is there?

All right enough, I have just a few days before I return. I need to be ready in the event it really happens. My hope is it doesn't happen, but if it does then I will deal with it. Who knows, maybe it was meant for me to meet myself. It may be interesting.

I don't know if something like this has ever happened in the history of this world, but to find myself the first or apparently first person to meet someone from another dimension or time is rather unique. Yet, there is an inherent danger in this meeting in this contact with another being from a place that is as totally foreign to this world as any being could ever be.

Behind all this was the greatest unknown of all and it was the reason for his coming to this place, this dimension. What was he up to? Was he a tourist or a spy? Or, was he there for criminal or some other illegal activity? The reasons for his coming here are as many as there are people living on this earth. Because of this, I needed to be alert and to remember everything taking place. I had this ingrained feeling it would become important in the not-too-distant future.

When I thought of that I decided I needed to wire myself as well. So, I headed for town and bought the hardware I needed to wire myself for recording any and all exchanges between us. I figured we would be together may be three or four hours and so I bought an external hard drive I could fit in my pocket with six to seven-hour capacity. It turned out they had only a ten-hour unit and so I went with that. The mic I would be wearing would be just under my shirt and it should pick up anything within a reasonable range from him.

I even installed a remote camera in my car and had it focused on the passenger's seat. What brought me to do that I'm not certain of, it just felt right to do it and so I did. That would turn out to be a most fortuitus move on my part.

Finally, the day came. I had gone in and started the recording system making sure it was on a refreshed start and then set it to run continuously until the other me left. I was waiting in my yard when there was a flash across the road. It was just after eight that morning and the skies were clear and it was going to be a warm day. It started as a ripple about four feet off the ground and then it appeared to form a bubble and the bubble expanded and seemed to explode with a blue green flash.

Sure, enough there was the car, well what I was calling a car. I have got to ask him about his machine or whatever it is. As I stood there, I noticed the door facing me was opening and a figure got out of the car. He stood there looking around and appeared to be testing the quality of the air or something. He was deep breathing, and just stood there.

I walked up to the end of my driveway and stopped at the road and stood there watching him. He finally stopped whatever it was he was doing and looked across the road at me. I raised my hand and gave a short wave and he responded. He then turned back to the door and bent over and reached inside the machine, then stood back up and closed the door. He turned and started walking across the field toward the road and me.

I watched me coming across the field. It was truly me, the same size and build. Same hair and skin color, all the same. When he got to the road he didn't stop, but walked straight across the road, all the time watching me and not paying any attention for any traffic that may be on the road.

As he walked up to me, we stood there and looked at each other. I started to say something and he raised his hand as a sign telling me to say nothing. He then looked over my shoulder toward my home and yard. He then walked around me and walked to the house and up onto the porch. I followed him onto the porch and when he sat down at the table, I joined him. He leaned back in the chair and then turned his attention to me.

He was looking intently at me, for what reason I did not know, other than trying to compare himself against me or should I say the two of us. "Todd my name is Todd Hancock, is that your whole name?"

Oh, brother is this going to be something to write home about. I responded by telling him, "Yes, that is my name."

He sat there a moment, "Todd may I ask how old you are?"

Again, a reasonable question, "I'm thirty-three years old and have lived in this house all my life."

He seemed to accept my answer. I didn't know what was going on at that moment. "So am I, thirty-three that is, but I don't live in a rural area like this. I live just outside of Wichita."

Okay, there was the first significant difference between our two lives. I continued to ask questions. "There is a Kansas and Wichita, where you come from?" It sounded odd, but who said there had to be the same places in his dimension as compared to ours.

He, smiled, "Where do you think I came from?"

Come on now let's not get funny about this thing. I'm confused enough and I don't need to have it get any worse. I needed to move ahead and settle into getting down to the real foundation of my questions. "I assume you're from another dimension, am I right?"

I was watching to see what his reaction was going to be when I asked the next question. He leaned forward as if my question was not totally expected. "Why yes, you're right. Do you move between other dimensions as well?"

Things were getting a little mixed up by this time and this question answering a question thing was not helping. Is it my turn to talk or is it his or, am I losing it? "No, we have never had that ability. Why are you here?"

He, again looked a little surprised at my response and question, "I travel between different dimensions looking to see different things and learning how I live in those different places."

Now we're getting somewhere. I looked across the road, "Why that big car and not something much smaller?"

He looked over at it and shrugged and looked back at me. "The size of the equipment and machinery is such because I need the car to hold it all. So, I end up with this car. Someday I hope to reduce the size to something less obvious."

All right, that sounded reasonable to me, after all our own growth into computers demonstrated that perfectly. "Aren't you seen by a lot of those who live in the other dimensions?"

I think I was starting to get his attention with the kinds of questions I was asking him. "No not really. I try to locate areas away from any large population. Your home here fits that criterion and so I parked in this field."

Now was the time to get a little more personal with him. "How is it you speak English?"

I, he looked at me. "In every dimension I've been to we all speak English. Some of the words are a little different and odd, but generally, it's all English. I always end up in another Kansas. That's where I start out from and I have ended up in one every time so far."

Well, I couldn't question that though it sounded a little off to me for some reason. Odd, but I guess if each dimension is a mirror of those next to it, then yes you would have that relationship. Yet, there were differences. He lived near Wichita and I live near Lebanon. He has the ability to travel between dimensions and I live here in this dimension in a farm house.

The subject material was becoming more and more personal for both of us as we continued our discussion. "Are there many differences between the different Todd's in those other dimensions? I mean are we all the same? You and I appear to be exactly the same."

He smiled and thought for a moment. "No, there are differences. For example, do you have a scar on your right leg just below the knee?"

Now that was strange. I did have a scar and he was sitting there showing me a scar which looked just like mine except. "No, I don't, I have a scar just under the left knee."

As I thought about it, it then dawned on me the scar placement was opposite from each other. I then started to watch his hand to see if he was right or left-handed? "See there are differences between us. I have even found dimensions where there is no us. There is no record of us anywhere. We just were not born in that dimension."

As he talked and moved his hands, I got the impression he was left-handed. The thing was I was right-handed. That caused me to really concentrate on him and take a good close up look.

"I have been to places where we are much older and much younger. Where we were married and had children and where we were single living with a woman and no children. So far it runs every variable you could think of."

As I sat there talking to me, I felt a strange feeling right between my eyes. I was developing a headache and knew in time it would move on into a migraine. "How many different dimensions have you been to?"

"So far, I've been to fifty-three different dimensions counting yours.

I thought. Wow, fifty-three dimensions that's a lot of traveling around between those different dimensions. "Are we all close to being the same between all those different dimensions, I mean are the locations, the physical surroundings in the different dimension, the same, or are there minor or major differences from one dimension to another?"

Things were getting all mixed up by this time. I thought I had organized my thoughts to some degree, but after talking to me for this period of time, it was getting more and more difficult trying to keep everything organized and rational.

There had to be a reason for his being here, other than just touring the Universes of every dimension in existence. Just what are you looking for or wanting to do?

You ever get the feeling something is not quite what you think is should be. There is a feeling something is off, not right, just outside the line, so to speak.

He was thinking about my question and then said. "At first I was just experimenting and then after successfully traveling to another dimension I decided to try and go to as many as I could."

This guy was either the richest person I had ever had the opportunity to meet, or he was being funded by someone else or some other organization. "Isn't that dangerous? I mean there are so many unknowns and if you stumble into the wrong location or have an accident what happens?"

This was wrong. There was something going on here, I knew I needed to be careful with what I said or asked.

Again, he considered my question. "Yes, I've considered it and so far, I guess I've lucked out. There have been a couple of close calls, but so far, I've managed to avoid any complications."

Someone, whether from this dimension or another just does not pop around all over the place visiting other dimensions, no there was something more here.

My mind was racing along at this time. He was too confident in himself and what he was doing. It was not like someone who was carefully maneuvering around so he would not create any problems within the dimension he was visiting. No, he was acting as if it was his place or property and not a place where he was visiting. It simply did not fit.

He then got up and walked over to my back door and went into the house. As I stepped in behind him, he was standing there looking the place over. He walked over to the kitchen sink and checked the faucet out, nodded his head and then turned and walked into the living room.

He saw my computer and walked over to it. He looked at me, "Internet ready?"

I answered. "Yes, it is."

He then walked through the rest of the house and then went back out the back door.

He stood there a minute and walked over to my car. "Wheels, that's interesting."

I looked over at his car and pointed out. "You have wheels on your car."

He looked at his car. "No, that's a cruiser and we stopped using wheels about thirty years ago. Those are actually resting blocks and are not designed to roll or to function as actual wheels."

He then turned to me and asked. "Could you drive me to Wichita?

I stood there not really knowing what to say. I was sure I needed to cooperate with him for the time being, and if we did make a run to Wichita, it would give me the chance to observe him closely and not draw too much attention to the fact, I was really checking him out. He wanted to go to Wichita, so I shrugged. "Sure, why not?"

Now wait a minute. We have a person who just popped into this dimension from God knows where and is walking around on my property, looking everything over as if he actually lived there. He acts as if it was his place, even when he told me he lived in Wichita. He was acting as if he was of a higher social position than mine.

Then he asked me, someone he just met for the first time, and I don't care if we look the same and prove to be the same, we are complete strangers. He asked me to take him to Wichita. No, this does not happen, all the alarms are ringing, and I'm going to go along with this? Yeah, I am.

Headache or not I wanted to know more about this person and this would prove to be the best access to the information I wanted. He wanted to go to Wichita and that was where we were going. Now I needed to continue to learn as much as I could about it. After all he was working to know as much as he could about me and Kansas.

We got in my car and as we got to the driveway entrance, he rolled the window down and pointed what I assumed was a remote control at the cruiser and it went away.

So far, my initial contact with this person had been anything but simple. It was like talking to a mirror and I don't really know if I have learned anything of any real value. I knew this, he was somewhat of an arrogant individual like he was of an upper class than I was and he was a person of great power and control. It was a feeling I did not like, but I needed to work around it and concentrate on learning more and not be offended by his demeanor.

Next, while I was studying his movements and actions, I noted he was missing a ring from his right hand. By the tan line I would say it was a large ring and would probably be something like a class ring. He had no wedding band on his left hand.

His clothes were well made and I would say, in this world, they were expensive and probably custom fitted to him. His shoes were clearly of the higher price range and again were made specifically for him. He did have a wrist watch and it appeared to be expensive as well. This could mean a number of things. He was wealthy or those he was working for paid him well to travel.

I then pointed out Wichita was almost two hundred miles away and would take about four to four and a half hours to get there.

He sat there for a few seconds. "Well, if it's not a big problem I would love to see it. We just need to drive there and then come back. I'm curious as to how it looks compared to my Wichita."

It was apparent this Todd was a control freak and was used to ordering and demanding others cater to his wants. There was no consideration as to whether I wanted to go to Wichita, he did and I was going to take him. The truth was I wanted to see how he reacted to seeing this Wichita, here in this place. I decided I was going to play the role of guide and see where this all took us.

Earth Todd, Me Todd, this dimension Todd, there is something going on here way outside of what he has told me so far. He claims to live in Wichita and he may be telling me the truth, but what is really in Wichita he wants to see. All right, I'll do it I'll go along with his wants and see where it takes us.

I agreed and we headed out. As we drove southeast, he kept a continuous narration going, comparing his Kansas to mine. At first, he said nothing new, it was a perfect description of Kansas as I knew it.

We drove through Lebanon and then on to Manako and then on to Jewell. As we left Jewell, his description of the landscape began to change.

Everything had been the same between the two locations but once they cleared Jewell, he noted a difference in the landscape. "Where's the Concordia Mountains?" He asked. "They should be right there ahead of us. It was actually a series of old volcanoes with an altitude of around five thousand one hundred feet. If I remember right there were ten of them running in a northeast to a southwest direction. It's just flat land here."

I looked where he was indicating. "It's always been this way. We are in the Great Plains and there are no major mountain ranges around here. We have a number of buttes all over this part of the country, but no major mountain ranges."

I noticed he kept looking up at the sky. We would drive for maybe ten to fifteen miles and he would lean way forward and look up out of the windshield. This went on two or three times before I finally asked. "What are you looking for?"

He looked over at me. "Don't you see them?"

I leaned forward and looked out and up. "See what?"

He pointed up. "Those things, those things up there circling and moving across the sky, they look alive, but how could that be?"

I looked again and all I saw were a number of birds, most of those being hawks. I looked at him. "You mean those birds up there?"

He looked up. "Birds, those are living creatures?"

I had to pull over, and I turned to him. "Those are birds. They are living creatures that can fly. Don't you have birds in your dimension?"

I could see by the look on his face he was confused. "How do they do that?"

I looked up again. "Fly?"

He nodded. "How can they do that?"

I got out of the car and walked around to his side as he was getting out. We stood there by the car as he watched the birds flying overhead. He turned to me. "Living things cannot do that? They have to be flying machines or something like that."

I stood there and then asked him. "In all the dimensions you have been in, what was it fifty-two, you have never seen a bird, a live, flying creature before?"

I stood there waiting for him to answer me and nothing came back, he just stood there looking at me and then looking at the birds.

This was significant. I could not believe he had been to all those other dimensions and none of them had birds. I could see where his and maybe one or two others would not have birds, but every other dimension bird-less? No, there was something wrong here. Either he had not been to all the dimensions he said he had gone to or he was just wrong.

We stood there several minutes and then one of the birds dropped down and landed on a power pole just fifty feet from where we were parked. He watched the bird with an intensity I had never seen before. This guy had never seen a bird and it was scaring me.

Just then a Pheasant popped up on the other side of the road and flew across the road right in front of us. It had landed in the cut wheat field just seventy to eighty feet away. He looked at me, his eyes were wide open. "That thing is beautiful, what's it called?"

"It's a Pheasant, a prairie bird they live in the high grasses around here." I replied.

Finally, he turned to me, "You asked if I had ever seen a flying creature before. I failed to respond to your question. No, I never have. In all the dimensions I have visited, this is unique to your dimension. I'm having a problem accepting the fact they are living creatures and not some mechanical device."

He looked back at the bird and then back to me. "Are there any other creatures that can fly here?"

I looked up at the hawks. "Yes, the birds are just one kind of creature that can fly, and there are many different kinds of birds. Some small, real small, and others even larger than these you see here. Other than airplanes and birds there are insects that fly, in fact most insects do fly."

"Airplanes, insects?" He responded.

All right, here we go again I was getting those same feelings again. He comes from a dimension that has mastered the art of dimensional travel, and he has never heard of an airplane or insects. I looked at him. "Airplanes are a flying mechanical device that is controlled by humans."

He started to nod.

I continued. "You got that all right? An airplane is a device that can fly, they have a motor or power device that drives or pulls them. It has wings that create an air foil that lifts the device off the ground."

Thank God for providence, just then I spotted a plane coming over the horizon and I pointed it out to him. He watched it as it came from the east heading west. It was five to six hundred feet off the ground.

As it came in closer, he obviously recognized it and pointed and nodded as it flew by. "Yes, we have sonic fliers, not airplanes."

I continued to answer his question. "We have airplanes, what you call sonic fliers, which carry large numbers of people from place to place. We have personal planes that carry from one to six or seven passengers, and of course we have the military airplanes."

He nodded at each type I told him about. Finally, we got that straight.

"Insects, what are those?" He asked.

"What?" I asked?

"What are insects?" He asked.

Great, here we go again. "An insect is a small creature, they live in the grass, ground, plants, or on animals. For the most part they are a pain."

Just then a bee flew by and he saw it. He pointed at it and looked at me with his mouth and eyes wide open.

I smiled. "That is a good insect. It helps in the harvest of our crops and provides us with a sweet food called honey. There are good insects and there are bad ones, the problem is there are many worse than the good insect."

I could see he was on overload by this time. He had seen two things that, in his mind, told him they could not exist, yet they do here. Birds and insects are new to him and he would need to work his way into their existence.

It dawned on me at this point as common as birds and insects were, I found it hard to believe they did not exist in some other dimension. If they actually did then he was not being truthful with me. He had not traveled to fifty-two other dimensions and in all probability, this was his first and only one. There was that warning feeling again, I knew there was more to this than he was giving me.

I walked back around and got in the car and he got in his side. I sat there thinking to myself. Now, that was one hell of an experience.

He had never seen a bird or insects before. That was just a little more than peculiar and I will need to think about it for a while. It just did not make any sense. No, I think I'm right he has not traveled as he said he had.

We continued on to Jamestown, then east to Concordia. As we pulled into Concordia, he looked a little confused. "We have no Concordia in my Kansas."

"Wow that's different. Why would there be no Concordia?" First, he stated they had a Concordia Mountain range as we approached the town of Concordia.

He answered, "I guess for the same reason you have no Concordia Mountain range."

"Yes, but we both have a place of some type named Concordia." I replied.

He nodded.

We turned south and went through Minneapolis and on to Salina. As we entered Salina, he started to get excited. "Yes, Wichita, my home town, it looks just like it." He was pointing out the most prominent features as we passed them.

I spotted a rest area and pulled in and

parked in the back of the parking lot.

I turned to him. "Are you saying this is Wichita?"

"Why, yes, it is. The skyline is almost a perfect match for my Wichita." He replied.

I sat back in my seat and then turned and looked at him again. "Here, in this dimension, this town is called Salina, Kansas. We are still twenty-five miles north of our Wichita."

He sat there trying to pull everything together. "No, our Salina is twenty-five miles south of our Wichita." This was a major difference he had found so far. There knowledge of another dimension was limited. I would imagine there are numerous differences in every dimension he had been to.

That's funny we have those two cities reversed between the two dimensions. I asked him. "What is your national government?"

He sat up and turned toward me. "In my dimension the continent I live on is The United States of America, Provence of the Commonwealth of the German Republic."

I sat there stunned for a minute or so. "The German Republic? What the hell are you talking about?"

He looked at me but remained calm. "The primary government of the Earth is the German Republic. It has been that way since 1946 when Germany won the Second World War.

"Within ten years after Germany had defeated the allies, the rest of the world including the Empire of Japan and the Italians became part of Germany. The capital of the world is Berlin."

I asked. "Is the Nazi Party still around?"

He looked at me puzzled. "Why yes, it is. It's the only political party allowed in the world and has been since 1948. It was then when all other forms of government were outlawed and we now have just one government worldwide."

I was still reeling from his first reference to Germany and then asked, "Whatever happened to Adolf Hitler?"

"Oh, the fuehrer, was killed in a bombing in 1947. It was when a huge bomb hit the heart of Berlin and killed him and his entire cabinet.

"General Franz Halder was then placed in the Fuhrer position and led the defeat of the allies and the rest of the world. After Hitler

76

and his cabinet were killed the party selected Halder to take Hitler's place and with that the rest of the world fell to the armies of Germany."

He seemed confused. "You seem to be a little surprised about Germany?"

Yeah, I was surprised all right. "In this world Germany and Japan were defeated by the allies and the war ended in 1945."

He sat back. "Wow, that's really different. I can't imagine a world without a united world government under Germany."

It then came to me. I looked him square in the eyes. "What year is it in your dimension right now?"

He kind of shook his head a second and then turned. "Why it's 2071."

"All right, in your dimension it is 2071. What would you think if I told you in this dimension, it was 2010? How does that sit with you?"

He sat there for some time thinking about what I had just said. I continued. "Not only that, but Hitler was killed in Berlin during the invasion of the Soviet Army into the city. He committed suicide in his bunker and then was taken outside by his loyal officers and cremated before the Soviets got there."

He got quiet and stayed that way, again for some time. I then said. "In addition, you have not only traveled from one dimension to another, you have also traveled back in time."

"No, that has never happened before. It has always been 2071 in each dimension I have found and entered." He replied.

Now he really looked like he was not sure just what was going on. I asked him. "What about all the other dimensions you had been to, what form of government did they have?"

"Each and every one of them had Germany winning the war and there being a single world government under Germany. In some cases, the Nazi party was not there and in others Hitler had never lived. But all were a single world government under Germany."

"You said this city in front of us was Wichita, Kansas and you lived just outside the main area of the city?"

"Yes, I live on a rather private location called Red Fox Lane. It's just off the end of Albert Avenue on the east side of town. The Lane circles three small lakes and is an enclosed residential area. The only access is off of the east end of Albert Avenue."

I started the car and looked at him. "We can go over and see if that Lane actually exists here in Salina, if you want."

He thought about it for a few minutes. "Yes, I think I would like to do that."

We drove back onto the highway and headed into downtown Salina.

About twenty minutes later we found Albert Avenue and turned east. Sure, enough we came to the end of Albert and it changed into Red Fox Lane. We then entered a tree lined enclosed residential area. There were three small lakes in the center of the neighborhood.

He directed me to a road running north and south between two of the lakes. On the north side of the lakes, we found one house sitting on the east side of the street, right on the lake. "That's the place," he said. "It looks just like my home, the same color and style. Everything matches, it's odd because no other dimension has been able to do that."

I pulled over and we sat there looking at the house and lake behind it. Even with the other discoveries I couldn't help but think about the government of his world. I had to pursue the issue. "What is the world government like?"

He looked at me and settled back in his seat. "Well, if you stay out of politics and obey the laws, you can live your life rather free of any interference from them. On the other hand, if you become an activist and are not a member of the Nazi party, you usually disappear in a fairly short time period.

"They don't waste any time on you. Their reaction is fast and brutal. So, everyone has learned to pay their taxes and not get involved in anything political. Do that and you're fairly sure of living to a ripe old age and doing so without any governmental interference."

"So, what's next with you? Do you want to go back to my home? Or, do you want to go someplace else?" I asked.

He turned to me, "I think I need to return to my dimension for a while. I have some thinking to do and I need to service my machine for my next trip back here."

As I put the car in gear and started to pull back onto the road I asked. "When will that be?"

He was still looking at his house and then turned his attention back to me. "In about three weeks?"

Now I had a chance to determine why

the schedule he had been following. That sounded familiar, so I pulled back on to the road and headed back to Lebanon and his vehicle. When you consider it, after each trip there was probably some maintenance process he needed to follow. In all probability any trip like this it could be hard on the person making the trip. He probably needed recovery time as well.

On the way back there was little exchange between the two of us. He was deep in thought and I was fairly sure he needed the time to think about what he had seen and learned. He continued to spend his time thinking about what he had seen so far. It came to me if he was here for some other reason he had to determine if he had missed anything.

As we pulled into the driveway at my home, he took his remote and pointed it at the spot where his machine was parked and it appeared. When I stopped, he got out and walked around to me and we shook hands. "I'll see you in three weeks."

I said I would be waiting his return. He turned, half waved at me, and walked to his machine, got in and flashed away.

Now what I have related to you may

sound farfetched, but that is the way it happened. If I had not been there myself and witnessed it all, I would not have believed it. The thing that got me was the fact he was so nonchalant about everything. Almost as if he expected me to do as he wanted and I was probably a little too naïve to really understand what was going on.

I knew I would be working overtime dealing with this past day and just what the hell he was up to. There was something wrong. It was almost like he was trying to keep me busy or involved in something.

Beside he had lied to me about the other dimensions he claimed to have been to. I could not believe out of fifty-three dimensions he had been to this was the only one, Dimension fifty-three, where he saw flying creatures.

That I needed to consider and do it now, right now. I only had three weeks and I needed to be ready for the next coming.

This whole thing had left me a little dizzy as well. Never in my wildest dreams would I have thought something as outrageous as this would take place. For a writer this was custom made for me. It was loaded with intrigue and suspense.

I could hardly begin to address all the possibilities sitting there in front of me. On the other hand, there was also a serious amount of threat involved in the whole thing. This thing was so unbelievable it could only be something that would happen to me.

I was looking at several hours of video recordings done by all the cameras I had installed. I knew most of it was empty shots of my property and the area across the 191, but the time spent on the porch and in the house would be something I needed to go over in detail to see if I could make any other determinations about this person and his purpose for being here.

That's what I expected but it was not what I got. In short order I had been thrust into a situation leaving me dumbfounded. I thought what had happened so far was strange and outrageous, but what was to come would make what I had seen and learned so far just a prelude to the opening of hells gates right there in little old Kansas.

Chapter Five

WARNING SIGNS

As I watched him walk across the field to his vehicle my mind started to mull over those things he had said about his dimension. It was a place where the Germans had won the Second World War. A dimension dominated by the Nazi party and no other political or activist activity was permitted.

Yet, here he was able to travel from dimension to dimension. It was obvious their technology was way ahead of ours. Their progress was sixty years ahead of us, so dimensional travel could be reasonable for them.

But the thing that kept coming back to my mind was the politics and the fact Nazism was the only form of government permitted there. It meant his social up bringing was in line with the political and social beliefs of the Germany of the nineteen thirties and forties. The foundation of their system was based on Adolph Hitler and his book Mein Kampf.

Now, I'm thirty-three and I was born in 1977, so I knew little about World War Two and the Nazi system of Germany at the time. I only knew what I had seen in the movies and on television, but what I saw was not too flattering toward the Germany of the time. It then came to me the next time I see him; I need to ask him about Jews, communism and Christianity in his dimension.

But, in order to do that I needed to know a whole lot more about the Germany of the thirties and forties, so I was going back to the computer and doing a lot of research in the next three weeks before he returned again. This time I was going to be ready for him and try to dig a little deeper into what he knew and what he was actually doing here.

There was one other issue that kept coming to mind and it was his real purpose for coming here. I could not accept the 'travel for the fun of it' reasoning he gave me. Then he said all the dimensions he had visited were single government and some were under the Nazi party of Germany and others were under different forms of government, but all under Germany. It did not fit right. The question came to me when did those other dimensions become a single government system? That would be meaningful to learn.

The one thing that kept hitting me was the fact he came here on his own, and what I knew about a Nazi form of government is no one, but no one, would be permitted to venture out on their own in this kind of activity. No, he was not an independent explorer, he was a representative of the government he lived under, and it could be no other way.

As I continued to research the Second World War and Nazi Germany I eventually got back to the Battle of Berlin. I knew the story of the battle fairly well, because it was one of the major climatic parts of World War II. It came to mind this was a key factor in this whole mystery and I needed to dig a little deeper.

It has always been assumed Hitler had died as a result of his own suicide and then had been cremated. At the time he had also killed his wife Eva and she too had been cremated with him. The problem with this whole thing was no one could confirm the bodies the Germans cremated were in fact Hitler and Eva.

My research had determined Hitler had used a number of look-a-likes during his reign and then I realized there had been a number of high-ranking officers of the Nazi Army who had disappeared and were never found. The other Todd had said the war had gone on for several years and Hitler had been killed in a bombing. The question was how did Hitler get there?

Had there been a Hitler in that dimension as well? It would be highly probable just about everyone had a double in some parallel universe. On the other hand, did the Hitler from our dimension arrive in the other one and carry out the conquest of that dimension? If he did then what would this mean to us today here in this time?

My mind almost exploded when the revelation actually hit me. The German Government under Hitler had developed dimensional travel. The records are full of all kinds of scientific projects they had been working on. Who says they were not working on an escape system by using dimensional travel as their means of escape? Was that possible? I guess it could be, but it would be a long shot and maybe there is no way of proving it. I had this strange feeling coming over me again. I knew, without a doubt, I had hit on the answer as to where the Nazi Government had gone.

Hidden within all the research and design for new weapons for the German Army, Hitler and his followers had slipped on to the means for them to escape being captured by the allied armies. They had developed, built and put into operation a master plan and the equipment needed to move from this dimension to another. The question was, had they made only one trip or had they made several trips to find the one place or dimension where there was no Hitler present in the target dimension?

Everything I had learned about the Fascist form of government told me they, the Fascist government, held an iron tight control over the nation and its people. Absolutely nothing could be maintained or pursued by any single group or single person without the government being involved. If they were, they would be discovered fairly soon and it usually meant their death.

This I knew above all else, the other Todd was not there on his own, he was not a dimensional traveler doing his own thing. He was here for a purpose, representing his government. If he was, then he was clearly a part of that governing body and carried a degree of authority and power himself. He may not be a high-ranking person there, but he was a dedicated person and one in which a great deal of trust was given.

Based on the differences I had discovered between his dimension and ours, told me this would be true for most of the others as well. No, there was clearly something else going on here and I was beginning to feel maybe I should not be involved in this thing on my own.

As with anyone else you tend to want to do something like this on your own. I guess it's a case of ownership, but in this case, it was clearly beyond me. No, I needed help here and I had better move on it and put the personal stuff behind me. Besides, I had felt the fear level increasing and this tells me something bad is coming.

But, who would I approach to help me? I knew a lot of people, both scientists and sociologists, who would have great interest in this situation. No, I would have to think about this for a while, however, I needed to act fast, and I only had three weeks to address the data and evidence I had accumulated during these last two meetings.

Then it hit me, Nancy, yes, she is an investigative reporter and everything I have experienced in working with her and read of hers has been great. Besides, she would know how to go about the process of pulling all the data together and researching further data and information we would need. Yes, Nancy, she was perfect.

Nancy Paulson is a well-known investigative reporter, journalist. She has a reputation of being tenacious and skilled in finding the details and verifying them. I have met her several times and we have had occasion to collaborate a time or two. If there was anyone who would be a benefit to this situation, I'm in, she would be the person. She would be the balance I would need. Someone who could weigh the issues and make the kind of decision this thing needed.

Nancy lives in Salina, but has worked all over the world. If I could get her to join me in this project, I would be miles down the road in dealing with my problem. With that I picked up the phone and made the call.

I was lucky, she answered on the second ring, "Hi Nancy, Todd Hancock, how are you doing today?"

There was a moment of silence. "Oh Todd, yes, I'm doing just fine. Forgive me for the blankness just then, but I've been working on a project here this week and when I get going, I tend to focus completely on what I'm doing."

I could see her doing just that, this was the most determined woman I had ever met, when she gets into something all you can do is get out of the way. I continued. "Nancy, I called you because I have a project I'm working on and I could really use some help. I was hoping I could get together with you and show you what I have and see if you're interested in it?"

This time there was a considerably longer pause than before. I could see her rolling her eyes and wondering what this guy really wants. We knew each other, but it's probably been a year and a half since I saw her last. Finally, she said. "Well Todd, I'm rather busy right at this time. I guess I could get together with you in five to six weeks. Things are just wild as hell around here and

I'm finding it hard to get away."

My heart sank as she was talking, but I needed to push the issue and then I had a flash of an idea this may be just the push I would need to get the meeting with her. "Nancy, what I have is something beyond me. I have video of what has taken place and I have no doubt once you see this, you will drop everything and join me."

That started her thinking and I could tell she was now setting everything else aside to hear me out. "Todd, can you give me any more on this? I mean is it something we can talk about on the phone?"

This time I paused and finally decided I needed to keep this from being compromised. "No, I can't go into any detail on the phone. All I can tell you is what I have here is something that has never been seen or has ever happened on this earth in all history. At least I believe it to be true.

"Nancy, if I'm wrong and you see I have violated your trust, I will understand if you throw me out. But I can tell you, you will not be disappointed. I need to see you in the next few days, any longer than that and this thing will be lost to us."

This time she came right back to me,

"Todd, how about tomorrow at your place?"

I almost dropped the phone. She caught me off guard and I almost failed to respond, "You sure about that? I mean, we could meet anytime in the next week if you want. But, if it will work for you, tomorrow would be great."

"Great, I'll be at your place, say around eleven tomorrow morning. Will that work?" By the sound of her voice, I was sure she truly wanted to hear and see what I had to show her. It appears my mentioning the videos had been the key to the meeting being set.

I knew it would take me all most all night to set things up for her, but I was determined and told her, "Nancy that would be great. I can assure you what I am about to show you will change everything we ever thought about the future."

We ended the phone call and I sat there looking at the stack of papers and video drives and disks sitting on my desk. Man, I've got around twenty hours to get everything organized and set up for her. As I was thinking about what I needed to do, my mind ran over the wisdom of bringing someone in from outside. But then I realized what was happening had to have a witness other than myself. For some reason I knew it was going to be important.

The next twenty hours passed like a charging bull. The next thing I knew there was a car pulling into my driveway. I walked to the door and opened is as Nancy was coming up the steps. We greeted each other and she came into the house.

For a few minutes she looked around the place. Old farm houses seem to draw the interest of people whenever they have the opportunity to walk through one. "Todd, this house is magnificent. I have never seen a home as beautiful. It is so stately and solid. When did you buy it?"

I stood there looking around the kitchen. "I didn't, this is the house I grew up in and my parents left it for me along with the farm. I sold the farm and kept the house."

She was clearly impressed with the house. It was a real gem of a Victorian home. "Well, you did the right thing, it's just wonderful."

Finally, we walked on into the kitchen and I offered her a cup of coffee, which she accepted. She sat down at the table as I poured the coffee and was looking out the window into the back-yard area when I set the cup down in front of her.

She looked up at me and then back to the back yard. "One forgets just how beautiful Kansas can be, until they see a place like this. I've been stuck in the city for so long I almost forgot what farm land looked like."

Then she turned to me, "Todd, I really don't have a lot of time, so if you don't mind could you tell me what I'm here for?"

It was interesting how fast her demeanor changed from visitation to business meeting. It set me back for a few seconds and then I knew it was time to take the jump and lay it all out for her. This was an all or nothing presentation and I hoped to hell I was up to it.

With that I started to tell her of what has happened over the last nine weeks or so. As I laid everything out for her, she appeared to be getting more and more interested. "Nancy, this all may sound like the ranting of a crazy man, and frankly that's just the way I have felt."

She was looking at the photos I had laid out on the table and then looked at me. "Todd, if these are actual photos of what you're trying to tell me, then I would say the most significant event in the history of mankind had happened here in this spot. What about the videos, you said you had videos?"

I agreed and picked up the first disk. "Yes, I do and I think it's time we looked at them." I placed the first disk in the player and she started watching it. When the disk got to the part where the other Todd and his machine flashed out of sight, she sat back and grabbed the table.

I thought she was going to fall out of her chair. She looked at me as she leaned over the table toward the monitor. "Oh my God! Is that real? Did that really happen? No, that can't be, there is no way that could be the real thing."

I had her. She was now committed and there was no way she could turn me down. "Well, Nancy, he'll be back here in another three weeks and you're invited to be here when he comes.

I have just one request of you and that is you write nothing of this down at this time. I want you to be sure and if you really meet him, then you will verify all I have here and all you have seen in those disks. Is that all right with you?"

I could see she was having a difficult time with this whole thing. She started to nod her head in agreement.

After viewing the rest of the disks and hearing me out, I told her the reason I called her was I had a bad feeling about this whole thing, especially when you take in to consideration the form of government from his dimension. Why was he here? That was the issue and I felt we needed to get something done before he returned.

Finally, she turned to me. The look in her eyes told me she was having a problem with this whole thing. I could see the soul of a journalist welling up in her and that caused me to sit back. I sure as hell hope I had not created a monster.

All I could do was to sit and wait. It seemed like hours before she finally put her hands on the table top and looked down between them. "All right, I agree with you reporting this situation now could be a real problem, both in trying to prove it and in attacking our reputations. However, I want one thing out of you and that is sole, exclusive and complete control of this event and its publishing."

Now it was my turn to sit back and think. When I first went into this thing all I wanted was verification what I was seeing was in fact real. But now it has become something else and I needed to protect my position or lose control of everything. She sat there waiting for me and I too was working hard trying to cover all the bases. The fat was in the fire and the only way to control her was to share it all with her.

I finally made my decision and looked at her. "OK Nancy, I agree. But I want us to work this thing as a partnership. Any story going into the media of any kind will be a joint by-line between the two of us. I can't stop you from publishing this information whenever you want, but if we're going to delve deeper into this thing, you will need total cooperation from me as well."

She smiled and picked up one of the photos of the man standing beside his machine. "Todd, this is going to be the biggest story to hit the media in the last three hundred years. It's going to take one hell of a lot of work and digging, but in the end, it will be the pinnacle of both our careers. I agree we work as a team. It's your contact and behind that will be my skills and knowledge in building a story and documenting it."

With that we had formed a team and we're ready to work everything up for the coming event. It was then she started talking about schedules. "Todd, I want to move in here with you. It will take me two or three days to get thing cleared up at home and then I plan on packing my things and moving out here until this job is completed. Is that all right with you?"

Wow, I hadn't expected this to happen. This could bring about some interesting issues in itself, namely, my neighbors and any talk about a woman living with me. I pointed that out to her and she sat back smiling. "Why Todd, are you embarrassed to have a woman living with you? Don't worry, I'm not going to be a problem for you and I'll mind my manners as well."

It made me laugh, "No, I was just thinking about the neighbors and any cover story we need to have to placate their curiosity. I guess I could say you are a cousin who will be staying with me for an extended period of time. That should work and leave us free to do what we need to do."

"All right then, I'm going to get the heck out of here for now. I will be back, say, in three days. Will that work for you?"

I looked at the calendar and then wrote it down as a reminder. "Yes, that will work in well. Now, what will you need in your room and for the work? I have a suite upstairs with a bath and kitchenette. If that will suit you then I will have it ready for you when you get back?"

"Oh, it would be perfect. As far as needs, I'll bring my laptop, but we could use another desk top computer. I'll also bring my own camera and recorder." She was writing these things down as she was going over them. Finally, she had it all organized and was ready to leave.

She got up and walked around to me. We shook hands and she took her note pad and purse and walked out the back door and to her car. As she got in her car, she looked at me. "Todd, this is a dangerous game we are getting ourselves into. With that, there are rules and those rules need to be followed closely. Rule one: Never talk outside our team situation. We only talk between ourselves and with no one else present.

Rule two: We listen to each other as we progress in this project. We will have disagreements, but we must always stop and listen to the other one's side of the story. That is vital.

Rule three: We must be loyal to one

another no matter what happens. Loyalty is paramount and comes before anything else. Understand?"

It was then I realized she was committing herself completely to this project. I knew her as a sincere and truthful person and when she commits, that is it. She just did and in spades and I was grateful, "Nancy, those rules are gold here. Thanks."

With that she left, pulling out of the driveway and heading east on the 191. I expected her back in three days and had a lot to do between now and then getting ready for her arrival. Just the thought of it gave me a headache.

No one had lived upstairs in the house for some time and so the entire area from the foot of the stairs to the farthest corner of the closet needed to be cleaned and cleaned in detail. It took me fully two days to get the job done and get a fresh coat of paint on the walls. When I was done, I was pleased with the results. It felt good to see the upstairs of the old house coming to life again. There were a lot of memories up there and this was a great opportunity to bring it all back.

In addition, I set up a new desk top computer in the den area downstairs and ran a hard wire for the internet up to her suite. That way we would not be using Wi-Fi and opening ourselves up to ease droppers in the event our project became public. With that I felt all was well and ready for the next day.

As I stood there looking everything over, I knew what was coming in the next few days would change my life. The question was whether the change would be good or not. I had committed myself to this project and our joint attempt to try and make some sense out of it. I felt a small tinge of doubt clawing at my brain and it made me wonder if I had done the right thing.

We had looked at a lot of evidence when she had been here and my feelings something was wrong were reinforced at the time. In the back of my mind, I had been going over all the data and was clearly seeing there was good evidence there was a problem with it. Not just for me and Nancy, but for this nation and the world overall.

Let's look at it this way. People do not pop in and out of dimensions like they were walking into a candy store. There had to be a reason and I was fairly sure in order to do what he was doing, there was a lot of money involved, not to mention the technology involved.

No, there was more than the other Todd involved here, and I would bet there is a governmental agency of some kind involved in his dimension.

It was a perfect scenario. Send one person across to contact their counterpart in the other dimension and from there gain his cooperation and build a landing base for an inter-dimensional invasion. It sounds like a lot of bull, but the concept is fundamentally sound. We'll see.

I knew this one truth. There had been a visitation by a person from another dimension. He had worked his way into a trip into the area of Salina and while doing it had taken great care in looking the landscape over. The way in which he viewed everything made me feel there was more behind his being here than I felt he was showing me.

No, I felt sure his purpose was that of a scout more than a tourist. He had reason for being here and his reason gave me a strong feeling of concern. It became more of a concern when I heard about his form of government, it sent a chill up my back and I have learned years ago when I had the feeling, to pay attention.

When Nancy arrived in the morning, we would have about two weeks before the next visit and we had to be ready. The problem was when I said ready, what was my actual purpose in being prepared for the coming. What did I really mean by the word ready?

By this time, I had a firm feeling as to where I stood on this whole matter. After talking with Nancy and getting her commitment and seeing her interest I knew my reasoning was right and logical. I wanted my meetings with the other Todd to be rewarding, but I also had to follow my feelings, and in this case, those feelings were genuine and needed to be recognized and addressed.

What was to follow would be both interesting and difficult at the same time. I had no idea I would get into this to such a degree. Before this was all over, both of us would find ourselves soul searching at every turn trying to deal with the emotions and doubts would be raining down on us.

But, most of all was a nagging feeling I was making more out of this than I really needed. Yet, there it was, a man had appeared across from my house and then flashed away.

When we met, he advised he was a dimension traveler. No, there was clearly something going on here and it was our obligation to try and determine what it was and what we should do about it.

Somewhere off in the void that makes up the existence between dimensions there was a place this other Todd called home. In that place there was an Earth, a United States, and a State of Kansas, none of which were exactly the same in all respects. So, if their physical makeup is not absolutely identical then it is only reasonable for me to believe or feel our personal existences are not identical in every respect.

It is that chance thing that makes this whole situation plausible at this time. As with the differences between that Todd and me, there could well have been a difference between there being a Hitler here and no Hitler there. So, if Hitler and his cohorts did in fact make the jump to the other dimension then they had to know a Hitler did not exist there at the time they jumped. It had to be that way.

If there had been a Hitler already there and another one popped in out of nowhere, I would imagine there would have been one hell of a reaction by the Hitler there when the new one showed up. Knowing all this is supposition I can only suggest the Germany of the 1940's here in this dimension must have made preliminary jumps to other dimensions to determine which one, if any, was void of a Hitler and then that dimension would be targeted for the Hitler of our dimension to jump to.

To the rest of those inhabitants of that dimension, the coming of Hitler, no matter how he showed up, would be historic for them however the hell it worked out. From my perspective this was the only way it could have happened. They, Hitler and his cohorts, had to know what was there in the other dimension.

They had built a dimension traveling machine and in doing that Hitler, in his insane like a fox make up, considered the fact, Germany, may well lose the war and if they did, he had better have some means of escape already set up so he and the others could jump out of this dimension and into the other.

It was risky as hell, but in his mind, it was probably worth it. If he couldn't have his world domination here, then he could jump and have it someplace else. And, I was willing to bet that is exactly what happened. That sly old fox had it figured all the way and if I were to extrapolate this line of thought I would have to consider the option he intended to reinvade this dimension down the line when he had a more formidable army and technology.

As crazy is this all sounds, remember it is pure speculation on my part, yet it is based on the facts as I know them right now. There is something terribly wrong going on here and my inner feelings are screaming danger. It's the kind of feeling, not only was your life on the line, but the whole of the world was on the line. As dumb as those sounds, it was the truth of the issue and I knew it. I think I better listen to them.

Chapter Six

THE OTHER SIDE

The machine appeared on the launching pad precisely on time. The maintenance team moved in and helped Todd out of the machine and to remove his belonging and data tapes of the trip. He walked to the edge of the launch pad and met his commanding officer Colonel Duane Miller and did the normal "Heil Hitler" salute and shook hands. "How did it go Todd?"

A smile moved across Todd's face. "Just great I got a good look at the landscape around my entry point and it fits well with our needs. They do not have the Concordia Mountain ranges we thought would be a problem. It is all prairie land and just right for tank maneuvers."

Colonel Miller was obviously happy with what he was hearing. "Well let's save the rest for the briefing session back at headquarters. I have a three-hour period set aside for that and then we can wait till tomorrow to address the next move."

It was then Nancy walked up with an arm full of documents and other items. She had spent three hours searching the house and working her way through all the files, records and computers in the target Todd's home. "Colonel, I found everything I think we need and I think we have a great location for the next big step."

They then moved over to the staff car and got in and headed off for the headquarters and the briefing session.

Captain Todd Hancock was a career officer in the SS and was looking forward to his first major military action. He had been raised in the Central Kansas area of the United States Commonwealth of the Democratic Republic of Germany. His father had been a career officer as well.

Todd had attended the usual schooling as a child and was determined to have the qualities needed to be successful in the military. He had been sent off to basic officer candidate school and then given an appointment to the SS Officers Candidate School. He graduated a second lieutenant and was assigned to a tank battalion under Colonel Miller.

He saw some limited action in the Dimension Forty-seven front, assigned to maintaining civilian control as the new Nazi government was set up in that dimension. The appointment to lead the attack on Dimension Fifty-three was his reward for his fine work at Forty-seven.

Nancy Paulson was a highly regarded special agent for the SS. She had lived in the Kansas region of mid America all her life. Her specialty was the collection and analysis of data and documents collected from the many fronts that were being carried out by their military. She was an expert on the United States and its civil and military branches.

Nancy had received her specialized training through the Office of Diplomatic Training in Berlin, Germany. She had scored high and was given the highest civilian ranking attainable at the time. She was on loan to Colonel Miller for the duration of the

Dimension Fifty-three campaign.

Back at the headquarters Colonel Miller called the meeting to order. He asked Captain Hancock to start the debriefing and would follow up with Miss. Paulson.

Captain Hancock stood and started his review of his contact activity in Dimension Fifty-three. The subject he targeted was the other Todd Hancock.

His first actual contact came as he was standing in an open field across what was called State Route 191 in the State of Kansas and about six hundred feet from the southern forty-eight states geographic center marker.

As he stood there looking the terrain over, he was watching the house of the other Todd when the target Todd actually came out the back door and stood there watching him. He had decided not to make actual face to face contact at the time, not knowing what the other Todd did for a living and not knowing if he had ties to the authorities in any way.

He returned to his machine and came back to the launch pad. He would need a three-week recovery period before it was safe for him to return to Dimension Fifty-three and take the next step in contacting the other Todd. During this run Nancy had been able to run a number of scans to determine the environmental situation there and the quality of the air and soil around the machine. Upon return, she too would need a three-week turnaround.

The next trip Todd had decided not to make direct contact again and instead made a sign he showed to the other man. As he held the sign the other Todd came out on the back porch and then turned and ran back into the house. Todd knew he had to be ready in the event the other Todd returned with a weapon.

About three minutes later he came out the back door again with a small camera in hand. As he brought it up to shoot a picture Todd returned to the machine and returned back to the launch pad. It would be another three weeks before the next jump.

In the third jump Todd used a sign again. This time the Other Todd was ready and brought the camera out with him and started shooting photos of Todd and his machine.

Meanwhile, Nancy was running the photo and video equipment and taking shots of the other Todd while he was photographing Captain Hancock. The captain was standing outside with the second sign advising the other Todd he would be back in three weeks and would then make contact with him.

Captain Hancock returned to the machine and they jumped back to the launch pad. Once back at the base they gathered in the conference room. With everyone present they laid out their plans for the next contact in three weeks.

The captain would try and get the other Todd to take him to Wichita so he could see his home there and see how different things were. Nancy would wait until they left and then would leave the machine and go to the other Todd's house and make a search for whatever data and documents she could locate. She felt she would need three hours to complete the search.

Finally, three weeks later they made the jump back to Dimension Fifty-three. When they arrived, the other Todd was standing in his driveway watching. He had his camera with him and was taking pictures as fast has he could push the button.

Captain Hancock got out of the machine and started to close the door. He stopped and held the door open with his left hand and waved at the other Todd with his right. Just then Nancy said. "Captain, take your ring off and give it to me. It may be a problem if he sees it and recognizes it."

The captain agreed and removed the ring and gave it to Nancy. He then closed the door and started walking toward the other Todd. Nancy was ready to make an emergency jump back to the launch pad if anything went wrong. That was the way they worked it. Captain Hancock would be sacrificed for the good of the campaign.

Nancy watched and videoed the meeting of the two Todd's and then the captain walked through the back door of the house and the other Todd followed him.

After several minutes they came back out and walked over to the other Todd's car and got in and drove out of the back yard and east on State Route 191. Nancy remained in the machine for another thirty minutes before she got out and walked over to the house and went in.

It was an old house, but one had clearly been well kept. As she looked around, she noted he was active in writing. As she went through the drawers of his desk, she found a number of notebooks and in two she found information she knew would be important to their final planning. She made copies of everything she felt would be of value.

She determined they had a fairly well-developed internet and then did a search for anything she could find on the military in the United States. It took her around three hours to pull everything together and when she was done, she left the house as close to the way she found it as possible.

She walked back across to the machine, got in and started organizing and recording the data and documents she had found. By the time Captain Hancock got back she had it all cataloged and organized.

As the captain got into the machine, she asked how it went. He sat there a moment. "Strange. It turns out their Wichita and Salina were reversed. The town I live in at home is Wichita, but this town here is Salina. I found the whole thing odd. When we found my home, it was exactly the same in every way. I think it really threw him a curve ball."

Nancy was handing him back his ring. "I have found just about everything we will need on this location and on their military make up. This dimension will be formidable to say the least. I think the location of our invasion is the best part of our plan. It will take them time to respond and I think we can move a lot faster than they can."

Captain Hancock was happy with what he had heard. "Well let's get back to the launch pad and then we can fill the Colonel in on everything we have found. I think the next time we come here it will be our first step in the assault."

Captain Hancock finished his briefing and then turned it over to Paulson. As she stood and walked to the head of the table, she was sure she had it all laid out. This was going to be a hard one, but they had the advantage of surprise and when a Blitzkrieg is initiated, it is unstoppable.

After her presentation, the staff personnel present appeared to be more than pleased with what they had returned with. As a result, they moved on to the planning phase of the Blitzkrieg. Generally, the plan was for the two of them Captain Hancock and Miss Paulson to return on the scheduled time and then they would have two hours to secure the house and put the other Todd out of commission. They did not have to kill him, just take him into custody and prevent him from alerting any one.

It had been determined the Colonel would go back with them this time and set up his command center in the old farm house. That would give him the opportunity to get a good view of the layout of the countryside and to complete the assignment layout of the tank battalions as they came across.

They had learned over time it was difficult for anyone to kill their look alike in the dimension they were invading. It was a psychological issue, but an issue they had learned through experience to avoid. The other Todd would be taken into custody and held in isolation until the commander of the attack had time to deal with him.

The next three weeks was packed with planning and mobilization of their invasion forces. They would gather the bulk of their tank force at the launch pad location of the invasion base.

At the designated hour, the Dimension Fifty-three unit would fire up the machine and open the portal. Once the portal was open then the portal enlarger would be initiated and the first of several thousand tanks and support vehicles and ground forces would start their invasion.

Because of the nature of the initial attack portal, their tanks would have to make their jump one at a time. That would require no less than three days to jump their entire invasion force to the Dimension Fifty-three invasion site.

In addition, they had nine other invasion forces set and ready to invade Dimension Fifty-three at the same time but in different locations across the world. As with past invasions of other dimensions their initial assault would be the same. If it went as planned this dimension would fall as well. It has worked every time and will this time.

There would be little rest for anyone. As the units entered Dimension Fifty-three, they would head out to their assigned staging points and then move out from there. With a Blitzkrieg, there is no nice way to do it. Everything and everyone are killed or destroyed in the first three days of action. The invasion force must make a one hundred percent jump to ensure full and complete domination of any opposing forces they may encounter.

In the initial jump there will be a crew who will set up a portal station in the new dimension. Their purpose is to build a larger portal so the Sonic Fliers could enter and then work to gain airspace domination. That would be vital and nothing else was more important than getting the portal base installed and on line.

Again, the location Captain Hancock had found, scouted, and selected was ideal for this type of a base development. When the preliminary information on this logistical location was provided to the planning staff, they were more than a little pleased. It was perfect and would greatly improve on their ability to strike and strike hard.

The small town of Lebanon was targeted first thing in order to gain control of the airport in town. As the Sonic Fliers crossed over, they would be able to advance to the airport and set it up as their primary base for the time being.

As the logistics and unit assignment needs were worked out and assignments made, the logistical elements were put into effect and the mass of support and supplies started to move into the jumping off point. It all was going like clockwork. This was a tried and proven process they had used in the prior invasions and each one had been totally successful.

Within the first week and a half the base was stacked with supplies, enough to support an army of over five hundred thousand personnel, three thousand five hundred tanks, one thousand five hundred rocket launchers, and a fully operational tactical air support force. All the logistical and support hardware and personnel needed to support an army of that size was prepared and ready for the attack jump. The same was true in organizing and preparing the other nine launch points.

During this time Captain Hancock, Miss Paulson and Colonel Miller worked together planning their approach to the farm house and the taking of the other Todd into custody. It was then when Miss Paulson asked a question, the other two would wish dearly they had taken seriously at the time. "I have been thinking about this whole operation and it came to my mind there could be a possibility our other Miss Paulson and Mr. Miller could pop up somewhere around that area. What do you think?"

Colonel Miller sat there a moment. A strange look came across his face. "You know, I have been involved in four invasions, the last two in actual combat. At no time did I come across my other Miller in any way, shape or form. It's not that it couldn't happen, it's just so far it has not happened and it has not happened to anyone I know who have been in other invasions.

"I really don't think it will be a problem and I think if it were, then we would deal with it when the time came. What do you think Captain?"

Todd turned and looked at the Colonel and reached up and ran his hand through his hair. "Colonel, I have no idea what to think concerning this issue. I've already been dealing with the other Todd and at no time did he mention anyone by the name of Miller or Nancy. In addition, I saw no evidence of either of them being around the farm house or anywhere between there and Wichita.

"The fact is Sir it never entered my mind one way or the other. I guess it should be taken into consideration on the off chance it could happen, but if it did, I feel fairly sure we'll be able to handle it without any difficulty."

Nancy picked up her note pad. "I just thought I would bring it up. I have no experience with something like this and I felt someone needed to address it just to make sure it has been touched on."

The Colonel was nodding his head as she was explaining herself. "I would say we keep our minds open as well as our eyes and if the issue presents itself, we will deal with it at the time."

Nancy nodded her head and then dropped the subject. "It would appear we are on a go for the invasion next week at the prescribed time?"

The Colonel smiled at her. "Yes, we are and I think we will be fully staged and ready to jump right on time. Now are there any questions concerning my being with you for the invasion jump?"

Captain Hancock sat there a minute. "No Sir. I think we have it all set and I am more than pleased to have you make the jump with us. My only problem Sir is we have several more days before the jump. I'm ready to go now."

"I know Todd, but our military is known for its precise planning and keeping of schedules. Its why we are so formidable." He had a smile on his face as he watched his eager assistant. "Everyone knows when and what they are going to be doing and we never change dates and times. It's built into us that way.

"All right, we need to get to the planning for the next jump and your actions in regards to the other Todd and his farm house.

"Todd, when we jump, I will remain in the back seat of the machine and you will go to the farm house and contact the other Todd. Please, do not kill him. We will deal with him later on. At this time just secure him and then Nancy and I will come over and help set up the operations base."

Nancy then reached over and picked up the map of the house and surrounding area. "Colonel, we have not addressed the issue of the other people who live in this area. By the map and Todd's observations there appear to be four other farm houses in the area of the initial assault. What will we do with those locations?"

The Colonel looked at the map. "I would say we will assign a unit to make a run to each farm and then eliminate the people at each farm. It shouldn't take more than an hour's time."

Todd was nodding in agreement. "We need to hit them hard and fast so they cannot get a warning out to anyone about our presence. We will have the other Todd under control and should secure our location until we have units hitting Lebanon.

"All right, now we're scheduled for the

jump at two o'clock our time. There is a problem we need to address. That is when we jump, the time will be close, but the number of years will be off by around sixty years. I don't know how this came about, but it is the way it is and our people will need to be aware of it, but not fixated on it."

Colonel Miller, put his hand to his chin. "Yes, I had forgot about that, you don't think it will be a problem?"

"No sir, I don't." Todd replied. "For the most part we will be running on our time and it's all that is important. Their time will have little or no impact on us. We are synchronized to our time and all we need to worry about. Any time adjustments which may need to be taken care of can be done after we have control of the invasion."

The Colonel sat there thinking about the time issue. He had never experienced anything like this before and felt they needed to run it by the scientists and see if they had any concerns. He made a note to contact the Office of Scientific Research and get their opinion on the time discrepancy between their date and the past date of Dimension Fifty-three.

For the next few days, they worked on

minor planning issues and running inspections of the advanced units and overall attack force. On the day of the invasion, they were set and all was in place.

Captain Hancock, Miss Paulson and Colonel Miller were at the launch pad an hour before the attack insertion. Each had their specific preparation activities and each attended to them with trained efficiency. The main invasion force was prepared and all weapons checked and support units in place. In the next hour a force never seen before by the Dimension Fifty-three target would hit them with such force the shear impact of the attack would disable them for a period of time.

Nancy Paulson had been to Dimension Fifty-three three of the first four times and she was comfortable in the preparations they had made during that time. Right now, she was concerned with doing her job and not making any critical errors. She had never been on an invasion before and she was a little scared as to just what to expect.

As she looked at the main attack force, she was stunned by the magnitude of the project and the fire power that was sitting there waiting to be unleashed. Yet, she was thrilled with the chance to be involved in something as magnificent as this was going to be.

Captain Hancock was in a similar state of anticipation. This was his first major action and he wanted to make sure no mistakes were made. He had worked hard bringing the data back from Dimension Fifty-three and there was still a little something working in the back of his mind questioning if he had done enough. He shrugged the feeling off and finished his preparations for the coming jump and invasion.

As they stood there a technician walked up to the Colonel, he was carrying a notepad computer. "Colonel, we have checked the time and date sequencer in the machine and found it was malfunctioning. It was this malfunction causing the sixty-year discrepancy the captain experienced."

Colonel Miller listened to him and then asked. "That may be the issue as far as the machine goes, but the captain also related there was a sixty-year difference based on his knowledge and experience. He was really living sixty years advanced over the Dimension Fifty-three location. Why is that?"

The technician replied. "Sir, during the

jump the process will cause the occupants of the machine to synchronize to the time frame the machine has inserted itself into. It had little effect on their activities and when they returned, they automatically resynchronized to our dimension. Sir it does not create a problem. What they need to remember is when they jump this time their jump will be synchronized to Dimension Fifty-three and it will be correct to our time as well."

The Colonel looked at Captain Todd. "Captain, do you understand what the tech has just related to me?"

"Yes, sir I do and it makes complete sense to me. In fact, I will be more than happy with things being synchronized."

Finally, the time for the jump came and the three of them took their places in the machine. As Todd started the jump process, they all belted themselves in. The jump was actually a rather violent experience for someone who had never done it before. That was the reason for a three-week break between the outgoing and incoming jump and the next time through again.

It wasn't a case of being thrown around or anything like that. It actually hit the cells of the body and disrupted a percentage of them.

It was enough to cause internal bleeding in some people. No one had been killed or died from the effects of a jump it just took three weeks to recover from it.

Finally, Captain Hancock pushed the insertion button and started the jump. The start of a jump was nothing to write home about. The machine started winding up and when it hit a certain power point the machine would start to shimmer and then fade away.

As they punched through into the other dimension it would cause a blue bubble to develop in the destination dimension. This was when they were the most vulnerable. The next twenty to thirty seconds would be a sit and wait time, usually it went uneventful.

Just as the bubble developed Nancy yelled. "What the hell is that?" pointing out the window on Captain Hancock's side of the machine.

They all looked and saw three streaks of vapor appear on Hancock's side of the machine coming right at it. Colonel Miller yelled. "They've got us. We're under attack."

Captain Hancock tried to stop the jump, but to no avail. The vapor trails shot right over the top of the machine and off into their home dimension. Just then they felt the impact of heavy rounds hitting the front and rear of the machine. Everything went dead and the machine dropped into its position in Dimension Fifty-three. It was dead in the water and they were cut off from the other side.

Then a third round came in the back-passenger area and Todd and Nancy heard the Colonel grunt and then there was silence. Todd looked back and saw the Colonel crumpled up against the back side of the car, his body nearly cut in half. The door itself had been blown off the machine and landed some twenty feet away. "Damn, they got the Colonel and were stuck like rats in a trap.

Almost as soon as he said that the window on Captain Hancock's side of the machine exploded inward and several barrels came punching into the machine along with several men yelling at them to freeze. The window on Nancy's side went the same way and more barrels appeared. They both stayed calm and did as they were told.

As they were being pulled from the machine Todd saw Colonel Miller running up to the machine. No, it wasn't the Colonel it was his other self in this dimension. The other Duane ran to the machine and looked in. He saw the Colonel and almost lost it. Who knows what it feels like to see one's self torn apart like that? From his looks, it was not a nice experience.

They were taken to the farm house and then sat down at a table and the other Duane walked in. He explained to them what was going on and then dropped the bomb shell. They had launched three nuclear bombs into the invader dimension and if they went off, which they felt was a high probability. It would mean the entire invasion force had been wiped out in one surprise move by these people in Dimension Fifty-three. Captain Hancock was heart sick and knew the end of the invasion was over before it even began.

For the first time in the history of the Nazi party their attempt to invade another dimension had been stopped cold. Not only had it been hit at the Kansas site, but the other nine locations across Dimension Fifty-three had been hit in the same way and just as effectively. The concern now would be the survival of the attacking dimensions social and political structure once the destruction of their military capabilities was complete.

You could see the impact on the two taken from the dimension machine. They were completely defeated and lost in the actions taking place around them. Who knows what this thing was doing to them at this time? I was sure both of them were mentally broke and it would take time and great effort to overcome, their emotions and the specter of their total loss.

Chapter Seven

THE INVESTIGATION STARTS

Three days to almost the minute Nancy pulled into my driveway. As I walked out to the car to meet her, I noted the car was loaded front to rear and bottom to top with things. I assumed the trunk was in the same condition. As she got out of the car, she looked at me and then back at the car. "It's just a few things I will need while I'm staying here, all right?"

"Yes, I guess so." As I nodded, I was thinking to myself, where in the heck, do we start emptying this thing? If I open the wrong door I'll die under an avalanche. So, like any smart man, I waited and let her open the first door. She did and no avalanche.

It took us around thirty minutes to

empty the car and get everything into her suite upstairs. I left her to put everything away and set the place up the way she wanted it. Meanwhile, I went downstairs and started to make lunch.

Almost on cue, she came walking into the kitchen as I set lunch on the table, "Great, just in time. Hope you like Caesar Salad for lunch." She looked the table over and nodded her approval.

We sat down and started to eat. "All right Nancy what's our first project?"

She sat there for a moment, "I think we need to get everything organized and then make copies of each and every piece of paper and audio and video disks. I want to take the originals to a bank, whichever one you use or want and place those in a safety deposit box. How does that sound to you?"

I hadn't even thought of that and knew then and there I picked the right person. "That works fine for me Nancy. I have most of the stuff organized right now, but I have not made copies of anything."

We finished lunch and then went to the den and started the job of copying everything. It took us four hours to complete the task and then we were ready to head for the bank. It was four thirty when we left the house. An hour later we were back at the house and starting to lay out our research calendar for the next two weeks.

By the time we finished with those two projects it was nearing dinner time. We decided to end the day's work and went to the kitchen and started preparing dinner. As we worked on dinner we started talking about the coming event when the other me returns for our next meeting.

"Todd, how do you feel about the past nine or so weeks and your encounter with the other you?"

It took me several minutes to formulate what I wanted to say. "Nancy, I am not sure as to just how I feel right now. When I first saw him, I went into a state of shock. We did not talk or meet the first time. All I saw was this man standing in the field across the road from my place. He was there only a few minutes and then he was gone.

"My impression was he was scouting the area. Looking it over, for what reason I had no idea. He popped in and then popped out a few minutes later. From that distance I didn't even know what he looked like.

"The next time he showed he had the

134

vehicle with him and again there was no contact. I guess if I had been him, it would have been the most logical thing to do. Check the area out first and then venture into making contact. But it raised my concerns and they never settled down.

"The next time he talked to me with a sign. Now, as I think about it, that was just plain weird. I mean, why the hell a sign when he could walk a hundred yards and say something to me. But, again, if I were him, I would probably have done the same thing, if for no other reason than to protect myself.

"Finally, he popped in and walked over to meet me. I had already seen him through my binoculars the time before and knew he was me, but what I did not expect was the way he acted. He was not mean or disrespectful, but he was aloof. It was like he was talking down to me all the time. He went where he wanted and never once asked permission. It should have started the warning signs screaming in my head.

"As we went to visit Wichita his description of the land while we traveled there was strange, to say the least. It's as if he expected it, but was surprised when he saw it. If I didn't know any better, I would say he was, again, acting the part of a scout. He took great pains in addressing the missing mountain range. He also took great pains in addressing the issue of birds and insects. The planes did not seem to be a big thing for him.

"No, he appeared to be a person, who made his first landing in a place where he had some familiarity with, but knew there were a lot of differences and was trying to get a feeling for those differences.

"When we talked about Salina and Wichita, he was surprised to see the two places were switched compared to his dimension. From a scout's perspective that would mean most of the maps of their world were wrong for this one. He was not happy, and appeared to be more concerned.

"Next, he has done this before. Just the way he acted and his demeanor told me he had taken this route before and knew he was going to keep doing it as he had before.

"However, I need to say he asked nothing about military issues here in our dimension. To me it could mean two things. First, he is here as he said he was and nothing more. Second, their military capabilities are so far ahead of ours, there is little or no worry they can overcome us with relatively little trouble."

She sat there looking at me for several minutes. The look on her face was a combination of puzzle and concern. "Todd, I have been many places throughout this world and I have seen a lot of war, everything you have said tells me this other you came here for something more than just to visit.

"I think you're right when you say what he was doing bothered you. It does me as well. I think we will need to be careful in our dealing with this man and I mean careful. I would guess when he comes this next time and finds me here, he will have an adverse reaction to me. He will not like it and will say so. Be ready for that and know if he does react then we most certainly have a bad situation going here."

It appeared we were set, finally. Now it was just a matter of waiting for him to return and then seeing what he was up to at the time. Up till now we had only concentrated on how I felt and whether I was in fact basing my feelings on solid evidence. Now the question was what was he doing here? For what purpose is he coming to our world and scouting it? We needed to do some speculating on that issue and so we got started.

I started the speculation. "Maybe he is looking for access to large amounts of valuable items he may start to ship back to his dimension for the purpose of selling them?"

She then added. "Maybe he was looking for places where he could market the technological advancement of his dimension over ours?"

It was my turn again. "Maybe he is looking for a place to ship those convicted of crimes in their dimension for serving their time here in ours?"

She continued. "Could it be they would just release those people into our dimension and then take off and leave us to deal with them? That's a fine thought."

She hesitated. "Could it be he is scouting ahead of an invasion of our world?"

I then remembered. "Come to think of it, he did mention something about sonic fliers. Also, this area of Kansas would be perfect for a military landing, if I knew anything about tactics in the military application. I have done a number of studies on tactics and their application over the years and this would be perfect for that. They could move a considerable number of personnel into this area before our military could even began to respond."

She was nodding her head. "What other application could be used by them?

I sat there thinking out loud. "If we consider the actual location he came to. He landed right at the geographical center of the lower forty-eight states. What could it mean to someone scouting our dimension? Maybe the fact he chose this location is the key to this thing. The only exception I can think of is I lived at this location. It may be with him being the other me in his dimension this would be the most logical place for him to come. It still could be just me he was looking for and nothing else."

Nancy had been sitting there quietly listening to me brainstorming these reasons when she raised her hand. She stopped me dead in my tracks. "Maybe it's not something diabolical, but instead something based on mercy. Maybe he is actually looking for you for something they are lacking there in his dimension, something lifesaving or even world saving?

"Todd, was there anything that looked out of sorts with him? By that I mean, was he healthy or did he have any obvious physical problems which stood out? Did he ask you any questions about your family history and your parent's health or anything of that nature?"

I sat there listening to Nancy interject those questions and trying to relate them to any of our previous meetings. "Wait, we did have a time there when we were talking about how we appeared in the different dimensions. He said he had been to dimensions where there was no Todd, in others where Todd was younger and others where Todd was older. He then referred to injuries and noted I had a scar under my left knee and he had the same scar under his right knee. But I don't remember anything specific about health.

"Wait a minute, there were things that drew my attention. Each time he got out of his machine he would stand there breathing deeply and hard. I thought it was just a control thing where he had to recover from the process of dimension jumping, or whatever you call it. And, then there were the three weeks in between, I have not been able to determine why the three weeks between visits."

I sat there centering on his actions while he was here and thought back to our trip to Wichita. There was a note of nostalgia there I had not realized before. It was like he had been home for a visit, not just there to see what his home looked like here. It was much more than that, far beyond just a visit for the sake of seeing something interesting. There was substance to that visit and it meant a lot to him.

I looked at Nancy, "I think he's dying. I think you've hit on the issue here. It's medical and not war. Their government may well be a single world government under the Germany of old, but it is not the reason he came. It's much more personal and involved. It can also be much more dangerous than we had expected."

Just then Nancy stopped cold. She sat there and said nothing. I leaned toward her and then reached out and touched the back of her hand. She looked down at her hand and then at me and snapped out of it. "Todd, Todd, me?

I sat there trying to connect with her. "What is it, Nancy?

Todd, me?

"Nancy what are you trying to say?" I was leaning in close to her now and trying to get her to concentrate on me.

"Is there another me?"

She then reconnected with me. "When he meets me, what will be the impact of the meeting? Will he know me? Am I the reason he is coming here? What is my relationship with him on the other side?" She then looked up at me.

We sat there looking at each other and not saying a thing, just looking. I thought to myself, if Nancy is here, she is there as well. If she has a relationship with me here, she will have one there. Just how close a relationship is, is anyone's guess.

What would her career or activity be there? We have no idea about that. It not only touched Nancy but I realized it included everyone I knew or knew me. This I'm afraid casts a whole new light on this situation. Now what?

So far, we've managed to muddle this whole thing up. All this guessing and speculation simply added nothing but confusion to our attempts to analyze this whole thing. There must be another way to address this issue and not end up flying off into some unproductive discussion that only takes our time, which we have little of.

How can we even think of others we

know and their relationship to us here and on the other side with the other Todd? It only opened the door to a never-ending case of speculation and add nothing to our issues at this time.

It was then when we started to center on a central subject. We needed to determine what it was we had in physical evidence and where the evidence was directing us. I had a table top full of audio and video tapes and disks and we had not even started to really review them and do some specific in-depth observation of what was there.

The issue of Nancy would finally bring us around to making the jump from speculation to specifics. With a whole new appreciation of what we were dealing with would emerge.

All right, we had our time of speculation. Now we needed to get specific and determine what it was we knew and did not know. That meant the videos needed to be looked at and not just viewed, but viewed from an evidentiary perspective.

All I expected were a number of shots of the other me walking over to my house and then walking around outside and inside the house as if he owned the place. Maybe, just maybe we would be able to find something out through his body language and mannerisms.

So far, we had wasted the better part of the day on speculation and copying of our records. None of it produced one single bit of data we could use to get a good clear look at this person and what his purpose was here in our world. Damn we have just over two weeks left and we have done nothing to put this thing together. Right then and there I decided we were going to concentrate on what we had and let it led us to a proper and supported conclusion as to what is going on.

I stood up and headed for the den and all the video and audio on the four hard drives sitting there. Nancy came behind me. As I sat down at the computer, I checked the time, it was almost seven o'clock. I then opened the file on the first hard drive and selected the first camera file and hit the play button.

As we sat there waiting for the computer to recognize and start the play back, I had a sense of excitement wash over me. I looked over at Nancy and I could tell she was feeling the same thing. She was busy getting pad and pencil ready so she could take notes as specifics started to appear.

We had a lot of records, information and data, but there was a lot of empty space on those hard drives as well. The first job was to determine which cameras would be viewed first and then next and so on. We didn't know it yet, but this night was going to be interesting and scary all at the same time.

What we didn't know was we were about to witness the presence of another player in this game and it would tell us the truth as to what was going on. But the greater if it all would be what was behind them as we looked through the portal they had just come through.

Chapter Eight

THE NANCY ENIGMA

Nothing is simple in this life and I guess in the other Todd's life as well. What had started out as a weird and confusing meeting between the same two people from different dimensions has now gone to an enigma which at this point leaves us totally unprepared and clueless as to what to do next?

The other Todd was a situation we needed to addressed and needed to have a determination as to just what he was doing here, his reasons and purpose for coming. But, with the addition of Nancy into this situation, a whole new issue or number of issues has been introduced. Namely, is there another Nancy on the other side, the other Todd's side? That question is quickly followed by a number of other questions.

If there is another Nancy, does she have the same profession as this Nancy? Is she currently assisting the other Todd in trying to determine the makeup of this dimension? If she is not of this Nancy's profession, then what is her profession and is it dangerous? The questions and doubts keep rolling out and driving us further and further back from the issues at hand.

The other Todd may pop into sight in two weeks and besides him getting out of his machine, the other Nancy may get out with him. Then what? Does this queer the whole thing or does it open everything up? We had to do something, but just what was the major issue.

I sat back and looked at Nancy. "Know what? I think I need to sit here and review every second I spent with the other Todd and try and determine all the differences I learned between the two of us. What do you think?"

Nancy looked at me for the longest time. You could see her mind churning away at the question. "You know what Todd; I think it would be a great idea. The problem is, how much can you remember at this point?"

Good question, but I was sure I had a handle on this issue. For one thing, I had a great memory for details. That has come over the years of research and writing I have done, and it was second nature to me. I mean, I'm the kind of personality where detail is everything. So, I decide to go for it.

I reached over and stopped the drive from playing and sat back and thought for a few moments. We needed to review all the drives, but maybe the first review should be my own memory of what had taken place. That should be done before we view the drives so my memory will not be influenced by what may or may not be on them.

"Nancy, I think I can give you almost everything we will need from the meetings I have had with the other Todd. So, if you can record, I'll start dumping and let's see what we can come up with."

So, I started recalling the several contacts I had with the other Todd. My purpose was to reach in and pull out every oddity I had observed including anything that brought about a question or caused me to consider what I was seeing and hearing.

You can never really understand just how the human mind functions until you're in a situation such as this. Recall can be a tricky thing, but when it gets started, it's a wonder as to how much you did see and how your mind brings it all back and lays it out for you.

In addition, when we start to review the drives, we will be able to match what we were seeing with my view of those periods of our contacts. It would give us areas where we needed to make close and detailed observations and comparisons to what had been recorded. So, the recall started and the revelations started to come forth.

"The first time I saw the other Todd, I at first, saw a stranger standing in the field across the road from my place. But, as I go back and take a close look, I saw a man with a purpose. He was not just standing there looking at the house across the road, he was looking at the terrain and the weather and the structures within his sight line. He was taking everything in, nothing was missed. It was a disciplined action, one that took everything into account and left nothing out.

"The second time he was in his machine and it was parked in the field across from my place in the same spot he had been standing. It was three weeks later. The other Todd got out of the machine and stood by it looking across at my place. I noted the fact he was in the same clothes or a matching outfit to the one he had been wearing the first time. Again, he was paying close attention to details. I noted the amount of time he had spent looking at the sky, in all directions. It was in the morning so the sun was still in the east and his machine was parked facing into the sun, directly into the sun.

"That visit had lasted maybe another ten minutes at the most. He then got back into the machine and left the same way he came." I stopped for a second and refocused on that part of the visit. "When he got in the machine he seemed to lean in and stopped like he was talking to someone and then stood back up and took a final look and then slowly got back in the machine and left.

"Strange, I had not noted that before. There had been someone else in the machine. I was sure of it now. Yes, there is no doubt there had been another in the machine."

Then I found myself zeroing in on the machine. For some reason I had not done that before, but now it all came charging at me. The machine, there was something distinctive about that machine. I had seen it before or something that looked very much like it. But what was it about that machine was drawing me in now?

What I had thought were tires were in fact blocks it rested on, but the design and overall size of the machine was the thing getting to me. I turned to Nancy, "The machine, Nancy. The machine is something I have seen before. We need to stop and go after the machine design, right now."

"Todd, can you give me a detailed description of the machine? We need something to start with."

I looked at her and seemed to come to a stop. I sat there for several minutes while she patiently waited for me to start. "Yeah, it was about twenty to twenty-five feet long. I would estimate the width at about a standard car, around six to eight feet. It was a low silhouette design. I would say no more than four feet high. It had four doors, a front windshield and a rear windshield. The doors had windows in them as well. All appeared to be darkened and you could not see through them. Nancy, it was a car."

"Todd, can you tell what type or make of a car it was?"

I sat there a minute and then realized it was, to us, an older model car, like one from the 1930s or 40s. "Nancy, it was an old military type vehicle, like a staff car, but a big one, long and low."

It took us about two hours, but we finally found it. It was clearly a vintage German Staff car from World War II. It matched the silhouette of the machine the other Todd was traveling in. It had been rebuilt to meet the needs of a dimension machine, whatever those needs were, but it was still the German Staff car I was looking at on the web.

The car was a 1939 Horch 930 four door solid top vehicle. During the Second World War it was a car used by the upper military element of the German army, usually of the Field Marshall Rank.

All right, we had a vehicle associated with his machine, but though it was old here, it could well be the most recent production model in his dimension. Still, we had a vehicle that appeared to match the basic structure of the machine he arrives and leaves in.

"All right, let's get back to your review of what you remember." Nancy said.

I then concentrated on the other Todd during this second meeting. "It was at that time I discovered he was actually me, well he was a 'me' from somewhere else, which I did not know at the time. It was then he used the small sign as I looked at him with my binoculars.

"I concentrated on the sign and then it came to me. It read 'Hi Todd, nice to meet you.' At the time I was so shocked I failed to actually see the sign. The lettering was done in Old English style, and it was bold print. My mind went back to the sign, it was hand printed, not mechanical. It was the way he wrote, or at least printed. Why that?"

Nancy was getting more and more excited as each new element of my memory became clear and I found each anomaly.

I continued. "That encounter ended when he returned to his machine and it flashed away. I remember running for the camera and then just getting ready to get a shot in when he was gone."

I was sitting there saying, camera over and over when it finally set in. "Damn, camera!" I reached over and picked it up. I took those pictures and never transferred them to the computer. The third meeting was on the camera.

I down loaded the photos and then

started to relate the third meeting to Nancy. "I remembered taking a mass of photos and then recalled the second sign. Yeah, I wanted him to come across the road, but he held up that sign. It read, "Todd, I'm from a parallel dimension. I'll be back in three weeks and then I will come over to meet you.

"Three weeks? What was the significance of three weeks? Between the first and second coming it was three weeks. Between the second and third coming it was three weeks. And, he was coming for a fourth visit and it would be three weeks. Why?"

So far, everything I had been able to remember and Nancy has recorded has only created more questions and no answers. Now, we had the photos to review and I hoped they would give us some answers.

I brought the first photo up on the monitor and blew it up to full screen size. I was right about the machine, it was the Horch 930 I thought it was, but it was also different. The windows were all darkened and they appeared to be thicker than normal. As I took a close look at the top surfaces of the vehicle, I could see the heat waves coming off of it. There was a definite ripple effect coming off the metal. So, the thing got hot while moving

154

between dimensions.

The next photo was the other Todd with the new sign being held up. I looked at the sign and it was clearly in the same script he had used before and it was also hand written. I sat there looking at the photo and the sign and then was drawn to the right hand holding the sign. I marked it and zoomed in. At double size I could see a ring and it appeared to be a large ring and stylized.

I doubled the size again and I could then make out the ring design. Both Nancy and I sucked a breath at the same time. It was a skull and cross bones ring of the old SS German military. He had not been wearing that ring when he came across the road to meet me and when we went to Wichita.

Nancy looked at me. "Todd, this has now gone from crazy to spooky and scary as hell. Why would he be wearing a ring like that unless he was a part of that group? I can imagine a few of our counter culture groups around the world wearing them, but someone of his stature and position to have the knowledge and funds to travel between dimensions, that's hard to believe, then having him removing it when he comes to meet you."

I then moved on to the next photo when

he was putting the sign back into the machine. "Nancy, do you see that?"

She leaned forward and strained to see the photo better. "What, Todd? What was I supposed to see? I didn't notice anything."

I marked the spot and then zoomed in at the edge of the sign and there it was a hand, a woman's hand. I looked at Nancy and then zoomed in on the hand. It was a right hand and there was a design on the fingernails. I heard Nancy gasp and I looked over at her.

"What is it?" I asked.

Tears were coming out of her eyes as she stared at the photo. She held up her right hand and on the same finger was the exact same design as was in the photo.

I felt my face flush and my stomach roll as I reached over and put my hand on her hand. "Listen, it just confirms the other Nancy is there and involved. That gives us the advantage and we can hide your presence until such time when you coming on the scene will give us the greater advantage. Hear me?"

She looked at me. "At least we now know the other Nancy is in fact involved. And, you're right it gives us a great advantage. All right, lets continue looking the photos over and then I want to see the videos."

The rest of the photos provided no additional information, just confirmation of what we had so far learned. We switched to the video files and would learn another load of surprises were in store for us.

We started with the field cameras first, the ones mounted on the fence where the other Todd's machine always came through at. I had a good idea as to when he would appear, if he maintained his usual schedule. So, I focused on the time frame he had to come through at, the exact spot each and every time.

Sure, enough a glow started to appear on the screen. At first it was just a ripple in the air and then a translucent gold color started to appear. We sat there watching this happen and it occurred to me to slow the video down so we could get a clear and accurate view of how this machine came between the dimensions.

As the color increased it formed into a bubbled area and then it cleared like looking through a bubble floating in the air. Nancy grabbed me, "Look, you can see into their dimension."

I watched closely and sure enough I could see through the portal and into the other side. The machine of the other Todd was sliding into view, but it was what we could see through the portal that stopped our hearts. It looked like a bunch of machines. I mean it was what appeared to be a large number of tanks spread out beyond the portal opening. Yes, it was a military force of considerable size.

The worst scenario was there before us. It was true, Todd was here as the leading edge of a military invasion of our world, time, dimension. This was quickly getting beyond our ability to deal with and it meant something more complex was in the making.

Then the other Todd's machine covered the view and the bubble dissipated and his machine was sitting there. We sat there watching the machine for maybe ten minutes and then the side door facing my home opened. We could see into the machine at that point and noted a panel of lights across the front of the machine and then another person inside, on the other side of the machine.

As he stood there it appeared the person in the machine said something and he turned and leaned over and into the machine. I saw his hands moving and then he reached over toward the other person. He then backed out of the machine and stood up.

He closed the door and stood there. This was when I noted he seemed to be testing the air or something, what he was testing for, if he actually was testing, I did not know. As he started walking toward me, I noted everything I had related to Nancy before.

He walked out of view of the fence mounted cameras and I started to stop the video and move on to the next camera when Nancy urged me to let it run all the way through. I increased the speed of the play back and waited till about the time the other Todd and I left my place I then went back to normal speed.

It was just about time when I saw the machine disappear. That must have been when the other Todd had used his remote to hide the machine. As the tape continued it then came to the point when the machine reappeared.

We sat there watching and the door on the other side of the machine started to open and we watched a woman get out of the machine. I heard Nancy say, "Oh, my God."

I looked over at her and nodded. "Feels strange to see yourself, doesn't it?"

This Nancy was exactly like the one sitting there beside me in size, hair color, style, and movements. She was wearing a gray uniform that was form fitting with a single patch on her left upper arm.

We watched the other Nancy walk around the front of the machine and then head toward my place. A she walked out of view I increased the speed of the video and passed through the rest of the recording until she came back into view walking toward the machine.

The time indicator on the monitor showed she had been in the house for about three hours. We looked close at her and noted she was carrying several items in her hands as she moved around to the other side of the machine, opened the door and then got back in. It was obvious she had been in my house and she must have searched for something and then took whatever she was looking for. It was then the machine disappeared again.

I then switched to the in-house videos and started to view them. I knew by the first field cameras where to move to and when I got there, she was just coming in the back door. She stopped in the kitchen and started browsing around, moving items on the counter tops and then opening drawers. I looked over at Nancy and she was riveted to the monitor as she watched herself going through the house.

The other Nancy moved out of the kitchen and into the office area off of the kitchen where my computer and writing works were located. It was here she started going into everything there. She was intent and dedicated about her work. I noted she was looking at my notebooks and then started the computer up and started making copies of several pages of my yellow notebook.

Nancy looked at me. "What is the yellow notebook for?"

"Those are notes on my research I did on the advanced weaponry of the army two and a half years ago." I replied as I watched the other Nancy finish making the copies.

She then started going through the drawers of my desk and again pulled out all the notebooks and started going through them. She stopped at the blue one and sat back and started reading, followed by more copying.

"What's that one for?" Nancy asked while pointing at the monitor screen.

I had to sit forward and get a closer look and then realized it was my notes on the national emergency response system for an article I had done two years earlier. "That is the National Emergency Response System notes."

She turned to the computer and went right into the internet. It was obvious she knew a lot about computers and the internet. I reasoned she would certainly have an in-depth knowledge of the internet and all computer applications being from another parallel dimension, and I was probably right. We could not make out where she went to, but she did print a bunch of pages on the printer and then closed the internet.

She collected the papers and added more clean paper to the printer, and then turned to the computer and went in and cleared the history of the internet search.

Nancy reacted, "Ah, crap. She killed all the history and we won't be able to determine where she went."

"Relax, I maintain a back up of all internet activity on my computers just to ensure I can back track if and when I need to. I'll be able to determine where she went and what she printed."

I turned to the computer and did my little game and it was not long and I had the locations she had gone to and reprinted the items she had printed. I pulled out the yellow and blue notebooks and located the probable areas she printed from and set them both beside the other items.

Nancy looked at me. "Todd, this has now gone beyond us. I don't know about you, but this needs to be seen by an expert I know. The problem is when he sees this stuff it becomes a federal issue and everything will be taken out of our hands. Understand?"

By now I was in the same mood Nancy was in and felt we were well over our heads in this thing. "Yeah, I think we need to move now and move fast. We have two weeks and a couple of days before they come back and there is a lot to do before then."

Clearly, we had stumbled onto something that was way beyond our situation. We were into areas directly tied to the welfare of our nation, if not the whole of the world. No, we had to get someone else involved, someone who knew about these things and could take direct action in dealing with what appeared to be taking place.

I had no doubt in my mind the other Todd was a scout for an invasion of this dimension. He had stated before he had been to a number of other dimensions and all of them had the same worldwide governmental system, a central government of the Nazi Party with Germany being the primary seat of government.

This told me he had not just visited these locations, but they had, over time, invaded them as well and had the same plans for us. That opened the door to my prior thoughts as to how Hitler had gotten there and how the Nazi party had taken over that dimension and then started its quest of conquest across the specter of time.

No, this was now much more than a wild story Nancy and I could convert to an article or book. It was the knowledge of a coming invasion that would tear this world apart and result in the slaughter of millions of people across the whole of the earth.

It was time to bring in people who had a greater understanding of what we had discovered. We needed someone who had a greater knowledge of the preliminary actions of any power in preparation in the launching of an invasion of our world.

No, what had started out as a strange and unusual event had now turned into a situation no longer involving just Nancy and me. It was far more than that, it had gone worldwide and yet it still was personal to me as well. It involved our neighbors and their families and homes. No this had to be taken to someone with the knowledge and know how in dealing with an issue such as this.

I didn't like it, but I knew better than to try and work it out ourselves. This individual meant business and it would probably mean our lives as well. Oh, one other thing, I was mad as hell with the other Todd. He had taken advantage of me and for that I had no feeling toward him or his dimension. As they have always said, "All's fair in Love and War."

He had selected war and we're going to take it to them, hopefully. But first we needed to get in touch with the experts on war to determine whether we were capable of dealing with this threat.

There was only one problem I had no idea at all where to find and how to contact someone with the expertise and knowledge that was needed. As it turned out Nancy had the exact guy identified and was ready to make the call.

We were making the right move, the only problem is, were me making it in time. It would depend on the person she was contacting and his willingness to come here and see our evidence. My greatest fear was he would refuse and then what the hell were we to do.

I was jumping the gun. We needn't worry about that until and if it happens. Right now, we had to call this person and get him to look at the videos we had there. What I didn't expect was the level of response he would produce.

Chapter Nine

PREPARING FOR WAR

It was the following morning and Nancy was talking on the phone and assuring the party on the other side we had national security information in our hands he needed to see. If he felt we were not truthful or our evidence was nothing then we would pay for his trip costs and his time. "God Duane, you've never been this difficult before. And, you know I'm good to my word, so why all the resistance?"

She sat there listening for a moment. "No Duane, this cannot wait for a few days. We are in a time critical situation here and we need you right now, if possible two hours ago."

She looked at me and half smiled and shrugged her shoulders. "Look Duane, it's not that far and you've gone further on less information than what I can and have given you. Let me say it again. We have photo and video support for our concerns and when you see it all you will agree. In fact, dear Duane, if I'm not being truthful about this, I'll do a striptease for you right where you sit, and I'll do it all the way."

She smiled and hung up and turned to me. "I tell you Todd, sex will do it every time. He's on his way and will be here by six o'clock this evening. I have to pick him up at the Lebanon Community Airport."

"Six o'clock, that's great and I'll go with you." I reached over and started straightening up the desk and office area, then looked at Nancy. "Is that all right?"

Nancy nodded her head. I could tell she was deep in thought. "What is it, Nancy? What is bothering you right now?"

She swung around in her chair and leaned back. "Todd, it's this whole thing. I find it hard to believe what I have been seeing, but yet I know it is real and there is a terrible danger facing us. I guess what is really bothering me is I'm involved. Not here,

168

but over there, on the other side. That is me there and it hurts like hell to see me involved in something as damaging as this looks to be."

I could understand her feeling, I felt the same, but I also knew the other me was a different person. "Look Nancy, yes, it is you and at the same time it is not you. That is another individual who happens to live in another dimension and has other beliefs and allegiances. So, don't go sending yourself off on a guilt trip when there is no reason to do so."

She threw her hands in the air, "Your right, what the hell anyway. We caught them and now we're going to stop them." She turned and started to help me organize our evidence and the place in general. "Oh, by the way, we'll need a room for Duane also."

Over the next five hours we finished organizing our information and set out to meet Duane at the Lebanon Community Airport. As we pulled into the parking lot, we saw a twin-engine landing and Nancy was sure it was Duane's plane.

Twenty minutes later she saw him coming into the terminal waiting area and got up and walked to meet him. As we approached, she reached out and gave him a hug and then turned toward me. "Duane Miller, this is Todd Hancock. Todd is the one this meeting is all about and the one who called my attention to it."

Duane reached out and took my hand looking me in the eyes. "So, you believe you have found something earth shattering?"

I nodded my head as I took his hand and replied, "I don't know how earth shattering it is, but I do know it is highly threatening."

We then turned and headed for the car. Over the next hour, as I drove home, Nancy filled Duane in on what was going on and how we felt we were in over our heads and needed someone of his caliber there to help. At this time Duane began to explain the situation from his perspective.

"Nancy, Todd, the two of you must understand I am a federal agent and anything you present to me from here on out determined to be of a national security issue will fall under my direct authority. It is vital it is maintained this way so we can move fast and directly to counter anything I deem a direct threat to this nation. Do you understand?"

I looked in the rear-view mirror back at

Duane. "Look, we feel we have run head long into something so far out and off base we cannot simply set it aside and forget about it. This thing is real and it is dangerous and it can only be handled by someone in your position. I don't know what else to do, we're at a standstill."

He settled back and turned his head and looked out the window. Nancy looked back at him. "What is it, Duane? What are you thinking?"

He looked back at Nancy. "When you first called and gave the information you did, it was limited and frankly sounded a whole lot bogus to me. I have no idea what you have really come up on, but just the few minutes we have talked I have a feeling this is real and we are about to be up to our ears in trouble. Nancy, I don't like what I'm hearing and I have a feeling you won't like what is about to come out of this whole thing."

As I watched Duane through the rearview mirror, I noted the expression on his face. It then came to me, there is something else behind this situation. Something knows and is directly related to what we are dealing with. It was just a feeling but a cold chill ran up my spine as I watched him. Yeah, he was right I was not going to like this.

By this time, we had arrived at home and parked. We walked Duane around the place, pointing out the camera placement and the primary area of concern we would be relating to over the next few hours. After the preliminary tour of the place, we returned to the house and went into the office area off the kitchen. We sat down and I started to lay things out for Duane. It was going to be a long night, but we had a lot to do and many questions to answer as well, I was sure of.

I started by laying out the history behind myself and built into the first and second observation of the other Todd and then moved on into the third meeting and the photos taken then. As I progressed along Duane sat there listening intently and looking at each item of evidence, we presented to him.

After about two hours we finally got into the real meat of our activity and started showing him the videos we had been recording. The further into the presentation the more intense and emotional he became. Finally, after about five hours I stopped and told him I needed a break. He almost grabbed me and then sat back nodding his head.

He was sweating profusely by this time,

and I could tell his mind was spinning with questions and doubts. Nancy brought a fresh pot of coffee and then Duane started to talk. "I don't know what you two have been up to, but if everything that follows is anywhere near as impressive as what you've shown me so far, I think I may have a stroke."

Nancy sat down and then turned to him. "Duane, what do you really think so far?"

He stopped in the middle of a sip of coffee and set his cup down. "Nancy, when you got to the first meeting with the other Todd, I'll tell you the truth, I was sure you two were full of crap. But as you progressed, I knew you were on the level. I wish the hell you weren't, but right now I really think we have a problem and we need to continue."

As I watched Duane talking to Nancy, I could see he was clearly much more involved in something than I had realized. It came to me this was not new news to him. How the hell could that be? I had to be reading him wrong, but the signs were there. There was something far more involved here than I realized, but I was beginning to see it.

Finally, we were ready to continue and it was at this time I decided to show him the close up. "Duane, what I'm going to show now is what actually caused us to contact you. I need to have you watch closely as I show these to you. I will point each issue out to you and then give you all the time you want to view them, is that all right?"

He looked at me. "Are they that involved or important?"

"Yeah, they are. In fact, these are the shots that scared us the most and we believe are a direct threat to this nation. It was, at that moment, when we decided this thing had gone beyond us and we needed someone like you to become involved. Duane, this thing is the scariest thing I have ever had the misfortune of witnessing."

I then ran the fence post videos and as the machine came into view it was preceded with the ball of what could have been plasma. With the full arrival of the machine, you could see through the plasma into the scene on the other side, in the other world. "Duane, watch this closely and tell us what you see?"

Duane repositioned himself so he could get a better straight on view of the monitor. As the video played and the plasma ball formed, he started to react. He leaned toward the monitor screen and then stood up, "Stop! Play that again." He was leaning on the desk top and looking at Nancy and then back at the monitor. His face had gone white and I could see his eyebrows angling down. His concentration was something else altogether.

I reran the same part of the tape and he leaned way over toward the screen. By now he was shaking and making the weirdest sound I had ever heard. "Those are tanks. My God, there are hundreds of them there."

I stopped the tape and asked him. "What kind of tanks are they Duane?"

He stood straight up and put his hands on his hips. He then looked at me. "Todd, if I know my military hardware, those are Tiger tanks. The same type of tank used by the German army in the Second World War, except they are advanced and appear to have better armament."

I looked over at Nancy and then back to Duane. "All right Duane, now I want you to see this. This is a photo of the other Todd standing in the open door of his machine. What I want you to take a close look at is the photo of his right hand resting on the top of the door. When he came to meet me the item on his hand was not there. It was obvious he had removed it before approaching me." I then put the photo showing the actual ring on his hand up on the screen and then zoomed in on the right hand.

He sat there and then I heard him inhale. "Todd, that is the right hand of an SS Officer of the German army."

"Now, I want to go back to the video and I want you to watch this." I then started the video and showed the other Todd leaning back into the machine and appear to be handing something, probably the ring and other items, to someone else in the machine.

He looked over at me and then at Nancy and then back to me and nodded his head toward Nancy. He was asking a question without his asking it verbally.

I replied. "Yes, there's another person in the machine? And you know who it is. You and I know this person and this is her double."

He was now wilting from the number of hits he had taken over the last few minutes. There was little doubt we had his total undivided attention now. He also knew we were not done dropping bombs on him.

I stopped the video. "Duane, what I am going to show you now is a video taken by my surveillance system while I was going with the other Todd to Wichita. Please pay close attention and understand, who you are seeing is not the person sitting here with us at this time."

I started the video and it showed the machine and then the door on the other side opening up. It stood open for a few minutes and then a person got out He reacted immediately. "A woman!"

Neither I nor Nancy said a word. We watched the woman walk around the front of the machine and over to the road and look both east and west and then walk across the road. As she approached the house Duane looked at Nancy, "No way. No way in hell. Nancy, that's you!"

Nancy leaned over by him. "No Duane it's not me, that is the other Nancy from the other dimension. I was tied up in a job out of state at the time this video was taken."

He continued to watch as she, the other Nancy entered the house and then started searching and taking items and finally leaving the house and crossing back over to the machine. "Todd, what did you find missing or disturbed after you discovered this video?"

I slid the stack of documents across the desk to him. "As best as I can tell, these are the papers she made copies of. She also carried out a search of the internet and tried to delete the history files of the computer when she finished. I have a special program for keeping a permanent record file of all history of all contacts made by my computer. These were the four locations she accessed."

Duane scanned the documents and each one addressed one of the four arms of our military establishment. The information addressed the size of each branch, the number of weapons systems in each branch, the type of weapon systems each branch maintained the estimated arsenal of every weapon.

Duane reached out put his hand on top of the pile. "I think she has tried to obtain as much information on our capabilities as she could in the time she had. I have little doubt we have a serious problem here and I am going to have to initiate an alert right now."

Nancy first looked at me and back to Duane. "What about Todd and me?"

"For the time being I want you two to remain here. We have one hell of a lot of work to do and little time to do it in. How many days till they return again?" He asked.

I looked at the calendar. "We have fifteen days before he returns. That is if he stays on schedule like he has before."

Duane then pulled out a phone and

leaned back in his chair and made a call. I sat there watching and listening as he contacted someone, who I didn't know at the time, He then started asking me more questions and relaying them to the other person. "Todd, how close did you get to that machine?"

I tried to think of the times I was contacted and then told Duane. "I got over to the gate on the other side of the road on the third visit. That would have put me about seventy-five to a hundred feet from the machine."

"Could you feel any heat or any vibrations or any effects from the machine at any time?" He asked.

"No, I don't recall any effects other than the sound it made when I was at the gate. It was a low hum, like an electrical contact, except it was a low frequency and I could feel the hum through my body." I recalled.

Duane paused for a moment. "You mentioned a color before, I believe. What was the color?"

"Well, the machine itself was gold in color. Now as I sit here and think about it the field that appeared before the machine became visible and while the machine was fully materializing was a light or hazy blue." I responded.

He talked to the other party for a minute or so. "When was the first time you actually met and talked one on one?"

"It was the fourth visit, I think. The prior three there was no direct contact. The first time he just stood there a few minutes and then disappeared. The machine was not even there. The second time he used a sign to signal me, and the same for the third time. The fourth time he did the things you saw on the video. He came across the 191 and we went to the house and then took the trip." I had no idea what they were digging for, but I knew I needed to be up front and give them everything I had.

After a few more minutes Duane hung up and looked at both of us. "As of right now, you are not to talk to anyone or have any contact outside of this house until further notice. There will be a large contingent of people here within six hours and at that time we will be making decisions as to what we are going to do."

Nancy stood up, "Then it's all right if I go up to my room and get cleaned up a little? I just need to relax and have some quiet time."

"Yes, that's all right, but first of all I

need to search your room and check for any cell phones or other electronics."

Nancy sat back down, "Never mind, here's my cell phone. It's hard as hell to be a journalist and not be able to report on something as big as this."

I looked at Nancy, "Hey, I gave you exclusive rights to this story, so relax. I'm sure they will not be talking about it to anyone and so you still should have the inside scoop on everything. Is that all right?"

She was nodding her head while looking down at the floor. She then looked up at me and made eye contact. Damn they were the most beautiful blue I had ever seen. "Why of course it is. I knew you would honor it, it's just that I'm used to getting right onto something and heading for the newsroom. But this time I also know we must control ourselves while this is being worked out."

Duane hung up the phone for a second time and then turned to us. "All right you two. This is what is going to happen over the next couple of days."

He had our complete and total attention. The game was now out of our hands and we were now under his direct and total control. No questions asked or any permission requested. He was in charge and we were, well, we were not. "We are going to have to go over this entire situation at least one more time and then we will want to do an in-depth search of the house and property, including the area where the machine comes in each time.

"My contacts don't like what they have heard so far and are fairly certain we are looking at a top priority situation. Nancy, Todd, the two of you, as of right now, you are restricted to this house for the foreseeable future while we work things out. We only have a few days before your friend returns and we want to have a little surprise waiting for them when they get here."

Things were quickly moving into another level and I needed to know. "Duane, is this a military situation at this point?"

He looked at me. "I guess with all the restrictions you're going to be living under for a while I can keep you informed. Yes, this is a military situation. The fact this other Todd comes in from what appears to be a military base, tells us they are in fact planning a military action of some kind against us."

At this point I guess I turned dumb or something because I popped up with one of the dumbest questions any one person could come up with. "Duane, how can you come to that conclusion by what you have seen in those photos and videos so far?" I asked him.

He sat there a moment, I guess to try and reason out why I would ask such a stupid question anyway. "OK, here it is. You are not the only ones who have had an experience like this over the last several months. We have three other situations in this country that are similar in nature. There are six others located around the world we have found and identified. The only difference is we are able to observe the military setting on the other side through your video and photo systems.

"The other situations were highly questionable when we considered the individuals. You have confirmed their situations and we can now progress. There had been a number of precautions taken as a result of those events, but still there were a lot of questions about the authentication of what those reporting to us had witnessed.

"We already have a protocol developed and a plan of action. What you are going to see here is a direct military special forces assault on your visiting Todd. Now, you need to be prepared for what is coming to your home in the next few hours. Todd, Nancy, this is the real thing and you will witness things you will not like. You must stay out of the way and only be present as a resource for information on the other Todd and Nancy who have come through the portal."

My stomach rolled. "God, are you sure you have to react that way?"

Duane looked at both of us and then leaned toward us. "Look you two. What you have come across is something we have been anticipating for a couple of years now. We knew if the other situations were true, we would be in a bad situation, but your situation has given us the opportunity to take a direct action and not be forced to wait until they actually cross over."

He sat back again, "Look, let me go over this with you. Maybe you need a little more information. This goes back to the end of World War Two when the allies were closing in on Germany. It was one hell of a battle. The Russians were tearing across eastern Germany and had entered Berlin. The Americans and British were holding the line in the west.

"When the Russians finally took Berlin, all the top leaders of the German army and government were nowhere to be found. The Americans and British thought the Russians had taken everyone of them back to Russia and they told them they believed it to be the truth no matter what they said. The Russians swore they had not, but few believed them.

"Well, they, the Russians, were telling the truth. When the Berlin Wall fell and the Russian government collapsed, the truth was finally found. They, the Russians, had not found any of the German military minds alive. At least they thought those who were found had been the real thing. The fact was, they were look-a-like replacements and the German power base had escaped.

"We are now fairly certain their escape was not to another country, but was in fact to another dimension, everyone, Hitler, Goring, Hemler, Goebbels, Hess, Bermann, Speer, Keitel, Jodl, Kesselring. All of them were scheduled to go with Hitler across to another dimension. They made sure they took all their technological knowledge with them and then destroyed the portal after they left. Subsequent bombing made sure the portal was destroyed.

"Beyond that, we have no idea what they were doing or wanted to do, but it appears they had a plan and it was to return when they were ready and take us on again. This time they have the size and technology to do it. That means we have to strike first and hard or else we are in for one hell of a beating."

I was stunned, if what Duane was saying was true, then we have been living in the Second World War all these years. The German military machine had just moved into another dimension and it was now launching a counter offensive against the world. That was scary as hell. "Duane how did they know which dimension to go to? I mean they just didn't jump across into some unsuspecting society and take over, did they?"

Duane sat there a minute, "Todd, we don't know the answer to that question. We have speculated about it, but we have no idea. One train of thought was they had made initial contact with the other side and found them receptive to what they wanted to do and that laid the foundation for their move. However, this is all speculation and we really do not know.

"What we do know is we cannot take any chances on this thing getting a foot hold in this world. We have to stop them before they make their move or else, we are probably going to get beat."

Nancy sat there. She looked like a little lost child as the magnitude of what was happening finally started to settle in on her. She looked over at me and shrugged her shoulders. "I just don't know what to say Todd. If Duane is right on all this, we are in one hell of a bad situation. I don't know, I just don't know."

She fell silent and seemed to drift off. I reached over and put my hand on hers and she looked at me and smiled. "I'll be all right. I just need to slow down and let thing settle in for a few minutes."

I nodded. "Me too."

I looked back at Duane. "All right Duane, what else can we do to help out?"

"Todd you can get the rest of your videos and photos set up and ready for our teams to analyze when they get here." Duane was busy stacking papers on the table into piles for future access, I could tell he was nervous and I felt he had good reason for being so.

It was then I decided I no longer had the privilege of just sitting around and watching things happen. I started to set things up and get ready for another presentation of the data we had so far. I turned to the computer and started to pull together the information I felt was needed on the whole of what I had learned and what was real here in our dimension.

That brought me to the terrain issue and I started to lay out what the terrain in this part of Kansas was like compared to what the other Todd had said. I took a stab at locating where the Concordia Mountains would have been located by the description, he gave me. I then went into the names of the towns as compared to the same location names from his dimension. I was somewhat surprised at the amount of information I had been able to gather while talking to him and making our trip to Wichita.

As I progressed into this project Nancy started to take interest and then Duane started to get involved. Between the three of us we had compiled a formidable amount of information by the time the first vehicle pulled into the driveway.

We first heard a vehicle turn into my driveway and we moved to the back door and went out onto the porch. This was just the first of a long list of rigs that would be pulling into my place and across the road into the fields there.

In a short time, all hell broke loose and the place went nuts. Every conceivable type of equipment one could think of was coming into the driveway or pulling into the field across the road. I was beginning to think I may see the last of my home and this part of Kansas.

Everything I had seen or read on the state of war told me at ground zero, the resulting damage to the environment and property was exceptional and I was surely sitting right in the middle of ground zero. I was getting sick as the reality of what was happening set in.

My mind went back to World War II and what it looked like as the different sides formed up for a battle. It was staggering as to the amount of equipment and troops that were used. What was even more staggering was what happened when all that might and power was unleased against each other. Yeah, I was getting sicker by the minute.

When it dawned on me, we were sitting right on ground zero and I had brought Nancy right into the middle of this whole mess. I was instantly so sick I was losing control. I looked over at her. "Nancy, I'm really sorry for getting you into this mess."

She looked at me. She was clearly worried and you could tell by her eyes she was scared as well. What the hell anyway, so was I. "Todd I'm here because I chose to be here, yes, I did not know it would come to this but I came here because I wanted to and I am staying for the same reason. You owe me no apology in anyway. All I ask is you not leave me alone when this thing starts." She was starting to tear up and I knew she was more than just a little scared.

I moved in close to her and put my hand on her shoulder. "Nancy, the moment this thing goes off I'll be right beside you and I will not leave you until we receive the all clear and everything is done." She reached up and put her hand on top of mine. I then said. "We are in this together and we will end it together. Is that all right with you?"

She smiled again and started to rub my hand and we sat there looking out the window as the military vehicles started coming into the back-drive way in force.

You can't understand what we were feeling as this thing continued to develop. That day when I saw the lone man standing across the road from my home, I would never have thought things would get to this level. It was all there. I couldn't refute it in anyway. This world of ours was being targeted for in invasion, the only problem is it was not a first-time invasion, it was a continuation of a long and hard fight that took place almost a hundred years ago and was now entering it second phase. That was the hard part, knowing this was still World War II.

Chapter Ten

FIRE BASE ALPHA

Within five hours my place was crawling with people. They came in cars, SUVs, trucks, and just about every form of transportation possible. Teams moved into the house and started going over all of our documentation, photos and videos. The place was a mad house.

I looked out the back door and there were no less than two dozen men walking around in the field where the other Todd's machine came in when he came to visit. I have no idea what the instruments they were using were, but there was a bunch of them.

We only had nine days to go before the other Todd returned and they were determined to be ready for him. The commander had arrived with the first wave of people advised they would be setting their priorities on capturing the other Todd and Nancy, when they arrived. Those two were targeted priority one and all efforts would be concentrated on that action.

Second, was the first strike at the military force in the other dimension? I had no idea as to how they were going to do it, but I could see they were setting up for it. What I didn't know was what they were setting up for was something that would hit Nancy and I so hard it would take everything we had to deal with it. It would be then when I finally came to realize just how dangerous this whole mess was.

I had been involved in a couple of research projects on our military and its ability to respond to a direct attack on this country. During those studies I had found just about every scenario possible had been developed and a contingency plan drawn up to deal with those scenarios. However, I had no idea as to whether there was a contingency plan that dealt with this scenario.

About that time a group of men came into the house. There were five of them and each one looked like he could handle himself. They gathered around the big table in my dining room and started laying out drawings of my place and the area across the road. They allowed me to be present as long as I stayed out of the way and kept quiet.

It was becoming clear they were planning on a double strike. The first to take the other Todd and Nancy into custody and the second was to launch a preemptive attack on the other side. It was that preemptive attack that caught my attention.

For the first time I heard the word nukes. My immediate reaction was not to believe what I had just heard. Then they said it again and I knew they were going to use nuclear weapons as their preemptive strike assault. But how the hell were they going to do that?

Over the course of the next three hours, I learned their plan. There were five of them involved in the plan, those standing around the table. The plan was for two to be carrying fifty caliber weapons designed to take out the dimensional machine the other Todd and other Nancy would be arriving in. The other three would be carrying launchers armed with the most advanced nuclear weapons available at this time.

The plan was to wait until the machine was on the ground and the entry portal was still open. The three with the nuke launchers would then launch their weapons through the portal and when they achieved that action the two with the fifty caliber guns would shoot the machine and knock it out of operation. The hope was when they did, the portal would close and we would have the machine here and they would have the three nukes in the other dimension.

The commander then said. "If we set the nukes for a wide spread, and give them two minutes time, we should be able to level an area equivalent to around fifteen square miles. In those fifteen square miles, absolutely nothing would survive. It would be total and complete destruction for both men and machines.

I found myself sitting down and looking at the commander. He looked over at me and walked around the table and up to me. He sat down beside me and leaned ahead and looked right at me. "I know it sounds brutal and maybe an overkill action we're talking about, but I want you to know we did not come to that determination in just a few minutes. We are looking at a situation, if they attempt and are successful in gaining a foothold in our world, we will probably not be able to stop them.

"As you were told a short time ago by Duane, we have had events happening all over the world with this issue and this is the only one where they have taken extensive steps to gain information about us and our ability to resist them. Todd, I'm afraid we are fighting for our very existence and if we don't cripple them now, well, they'll kill us next."

I knew he was right. It was just the fact the term nuke carried such a terrible connotation to it. "Commander, I do understand what you're saying and it is more than likely the right and correct decision that must be made. But it still is hard to take and difficult to accept. I hope you understand my feelings in this."

He was looking at the floor and nodding his head as I was talking to him. When I finished, he turned his head toward me and sat there looking at me for several seconds. "Todd, I completely understand and believe me when I tell you when the decision was finally made, I had the same feelings and had the same difficulty in accepting the necessity of this action.

"I'm military and you would think the use of any weapon was not that big a deal for someone in a career position in the military. I must say it is not true. When this decision was made, every individual around the table, and that included the President of our country had a difficult time making it.

"I know each and every one of those twenty-six people and to the person, they didn't like even the thought of what was being planned. But they also knew if we didn't stop them, they would come into our world and they would win, there was no question about it. So, we made the decision and now it's come to this and its real."

Over the course of the next few days the amount of military activity taking place around my home was unbelievable. There was no way any adversary could have come into that area and carried out any form of an attack successfully. They were going to plug the hole in our dike and do it permanently. It was just that simple and just that brutal.

It then came to me my neighbors were probably in the same situation we were. When I checked, I was advised all the neighbors within ten miles had been evacuated to holding camps and isolated so no information on this activity at my home got out of this area. In addition, a national no fly zone had been set up over this part of Kansas and was being enforced by the Air Force. There was a total lock down for twenty miles in every direction.

Five days later as I got up from the kitchen table and started to walk away, I saw a green van pull into the back-garage area and park in the middle of the driveway. Immediately a contingency of men, fully armed, moved in and around the van and turned so they were facing outward. I knew instinctively the nukes were in that van.

The first thought that hit me was the fact they had brought the weapon here in just one little van and with no physically present protection of any kind. As I thought about it, this was probably the best method in the long run. It's a simple green van and would probably be seen by others as just that.

The strike team which had been spending most of their time at the dining room table set their paper work down, got up and walked out to the van. The back door opened and two of them entered and started handing metal crates out to the other three. They then took the cases into the barn and closed the doors. The armed unit then moved over to the barn and moved into positions at the doors and each corner of the building.

At this time my attention was drawn to Nancy and Duane in the office area off of the kitchen. I walked over to them and they invited me to sit down. At the same time the Commander walked up and took the fourth chair and sat down. Duane then said. "Todd, I have been asked to fill the two of you in on what is going to take place here in four days. We feel you need to know so you will be able to assist us as we carry out our actions.

"Todd the assault teams you were with during the briefing and planning will move into their assigned places about two hours before the arrival of the other Todd and Nancy. The two gunners will be on the outside of the deployment layout. Their job is to take the machine out when it becomes fully present in our dimension.

"They will do that by shooting fifty caliber rounds through the front end and rear end areas of the machine. The gunner on the right will put a third round through the back-seat area of the machine. The objective being to cripple or knock the drive capabilities of the machine out, leaving it stranded here in our dimension.

"Almost at the same time the three nuke shooters will concentrate on putting their weapons through the portal when the view into the other dimension is at full viewing levels and the portal is fully open. In effect the machine will be coming into our dimension at almost the same time the nukes will be traveling pass them and into their dimension.

"It's a time critical situation and must be done right the first time. There will be no second chances in this one. The weapons are set to separate after traveling approximately five hundred yards into the other dimension and turn for altitude. Altitude is the key to these weapons and they must hit fifteen hundred feet before they detonate.

"The impact of one weapon will be equivalent to about fifty megatons of TNT. The three weapons will be enough to completely wipe out an area of thirty-five to fifty-five square miles around the epicenter. It will be total destruction. On top of that the electromagnetic pulse will literally destroy any and all electronics within a sixty-to-seventy-mile radius.

"The thermal radiation will range out as far as sixty miles from the center of the impact zone. The three weapons will complement each other and force the destruction impact well beyond that of a single weapon. Whatever the location and size of the base, it will generally be knocked completely out of action, probably total destruction.

"That will not eliminate their danger to us, but it will give them a message and hopefully they will think twice before venturing any further in carrying out an attack against us."

I sat there and listened closely to what Duane had to say and then turned to the Commander. "Commander, as I understand it, you have detected other locations in this country and across the world where they have made contact with people in our dimension, is that right?"

He nodded his head. "Yes, that is true."

"Then, would it not be reasonable to think if we hit them at this portal, they would have the capabilities of hitting us back at anyone or all of the other locations you have identified so far?"

He sat there working up his answer.

"We had thought about that Todd, and we feel we must make a statement first thing right off the bat. Besides what is taking place here, the same assault action will take place in the other nine locations. In fact, it means a total of thirty nuclear devices will be delivered into their dimension all at the same time. That will be a total of fifteen hundred megatons of TNT going off in their dimension. We had to be ready if they attack through all locations. If not, only those where they attack from will be hit.

We are anticipating a total knockout punch in this one assault. We simply have no choice; we have to hit them a killing blow or we leave ourselves open for a counter attack and that must not happen. The amount of damage to life and property, if all the tonnage had gone off in this world, would be cataclysmic. We cannot sustain a war with them over the long haul. We must end it fast and decisively.

"The Germans were well known for their Blitzkrieg attacks and there is no reason to believe they would not come at us in the same way now. No, we feel the first to hit is the one who has the greatest probability of coming out of this thing the victor. Anything less would mean total and utter defeat."

All I could do was sit there and think about what he had just said. It was rational and probably tactically correct, but the thought of all those beings dying on the other side still hurt me deeply. I couldn't blame or accuse our people for their combined choice of action. I understood and, in reality, it is probably the right thing to do.

Still, I had feelings about what was going to happen in the other dimension. "Well Commander, I'm not sitting here accusing you of doing anything wrong. I understand what you're facing and it is probably the right way to go. I'm not used to this kind of decision making and I guess I carry a degree of guilt within me as well. So, if there is anything I can do to help or provide you with additional research or whatever, please let me know."

He stood up and turned and looked down on me, "Todd, thank you for your understanding. These are not easy decisions we have to make and, yes, we too wonder if we are making the right decision, and there is a degree of guilt we carry with us. I know what these weapons can do and I hate the idea of them being used, but my job is this nation and this world and its security and for that I am willing to take whatever steps are needed to try to insure our survival."

With that he turned and walked through the kitchen and out the back door. I stood up and walked over to the kitchen door and stood there watching him walking across to the barn and then through the door. I had seen the look in his eyes and I could tell he was having a hard time with this whole thing. I knew then we were in good hands.

The actions around the farm increased as we drew closer to the day of the other Todd's return. Many of the vehicles and other equipment that had been parked all around the area were moved out of sight and the place was put back into its normal appearance. They had built special blinds in the field across from the driveway and surrounding the location where the other Todd's machine would land.

Fire Base Alpha was set up and ready for action. This would be the first and most critical action taken in the defense of our nation from an inter-dimensional conflict. Whether this developed into a full-blown worldwide war, we had no way of knowing, but there was one thing that was certain, we were going to send them one hell of a message.

On that day, there could be ten-dimension machines landing on this world, and at the same time thirty nuclear devices would streak through those ten portals and into the other dimension, and fifteen hundred megatons of pure hell would be unleashed. We wouldn't see it or hear it, but if it worked, we would be free from any future attempts to invade this dimension, at least for the foreseeable future.

The next three days were crazy. I don't know how many personnel the military had at the farm, but there were a bunch of them. It appeared they were divided into groups and each and every group had something to do or someplace to go while preparing for the coming action.

As I watched them prepare, I saw whatever they were doing they took great care in not changing the outward appearance of the farm and house. Nothing was left to chance. Every single item was carefully put back in its place, if it had been moved for any reason. I thought to myself, just how amazing it was to have that many people present doing I don't know how many different things, and they left everything just as they found it.

As I said before, they had gone around to the several farms and homes near my place and moved the families out and to safety. They were not advised as to what was going on or why they were being moved, they were being moved and they had nothing to say about it. In addition, they were not allowed to contact anyone in any way. Basically, they were kidnapped and moved away.

Then the town of Lebanon was isolated with all their communications capabilities knocked out and the town further isolated with road blocks on each and every road leaving the town, no one was being allowed outside the area.

There were a lot of angry people and they were not given any information as to what was happening. They were advised if they attempted to leave and managed to get outside the containment area, they would be fired on with the full intention of killing them. In effect they were being told stay put or die.

I was still trying to deal with the fact the past can still come back and bite us so many years later. I like most other Americans who never personally witnessed the Second World War, had seen many films and studies on the war and the massive battles that took place.

When we looked at the pictures of the towns and cities that had been sitting in the path of these huge battles, we could hardly believe the damage and destruction brought upon those who lived in those cities. You cannot imagine the pain, the terror they felt when these battles rolled through their homes and towns.

Now, it was going to start all over again if this preemptive strike did not work, and it would be coming from my farm. Then it hit me, if they came and were successful, I would know nothing about it. You don't live at ground zero of an event like this and expect to be alive when it moves on. I would witness little of it and then die.

That, I can assure you, put a whole new perspective on this situation and what was going to happen in a little over a day from now. I looked over at Nancy and felt a sudden sadness as I watched her going over a pile of papers. She would be gone too and the other Todd and Nancy would take our place and live our lives and I was not going to give in to them, no way.

That's it, we have a choice, and depending on that choice we will either live or die and know what, I preferred to live and if anyone were to die, then it was going to be them and not us. Believe me, once you see the alternatives, you find little difficulty in seeing the other guy die instead of you.

As I watched the final preparations for the coming event I was impressed with the mannerism of the military personnel as they went about their preparations. Surely, they were concerned for their own safety, but they still did their jobs and worked toward achieving their desired goals.

It was then I started to think about those who would be on the front line, carrying out the assigned duties they had been given. To be the ones who would shoot the nukes into the other dimension had to be more than a little stressful. Not only were they going to shoot them into the other dimension, but when they went off it would kill an untold number of beings.

Then I thought what if they missed the portal, what would happen? The obvious answer was a nuclear explosion right dead center in the continental United States. Crap, now I was really scared with the realization as to the size of the gamble being taken by these people in order to stop this invasion, right here and right now.

I had a whole new perspective of this situation now and I knew I had to be sure to not be the cause of any friction or difficulties for those who were saddled with this huge responsibility.

We were approaching the final day and people were rechecking and triple checking their jobs and equipment to insure the best possible performance of each and every one of them. Nancy and I were still in a holding position, which in many respects was harder than those who had a job to do. All we could do was sit and wait and think and anticipate what was to come.

How could this have come about? True it was not of our doing, but still I felt, and I'm sure Nancy did as well, a degree of responsibility for what was about to happen on Earth in one day. That is the Earth of the other dimension.

The only issue that seemed to cling to my mind was the specter of a possible missed shot with one of the rockets. That would end it all for us as well.

Finally, Nancy reached over and touched me. She had been watching me for some time and could tell I was in a struggle over all that was happening here at my home. She then said. "Listen to me, there is nothing you can do about what is happening here. The fact is there has been nothing you could have done at any time during this whole situation. Even if you had challenged the other Todd, it still would have been a war on either side of the portal or both. Do not take the responsibility for the whole of this event. It's simply not yours."

She was right and I knew it, but there was still this feeling of being involved in something totally against my nature. And, now Nancy was involved. As I looked at her, I began to realize I had more than just friendship feeling toward her. I was falling in love and doing it at exactly the wrong time in our relationship.

It was finally sinking in as I looked at her, I saw more than just a woman sitting there. I was seeing a person who matched my soul in every detail. I didn't know how she felt, but for me this was the most important woman in my life. I decided then and there, if we survive this thing, I was going to make every effort possible to address our relationship.

This is one hell of a time to think about

love. We were on the cusp of bring total hell upon a perceived enemy and in the form of a nuclear holocaust the likes of which they probably have never seen before. If their Earth was anything near what ours was, I found it hard to see the introduction of nuclear destruction into their world and lives.

Well, the game plans were set and nothing was going to change, unless the others, the Nazi's on the other side had a change of heart, which I knew was highly unlikely. This thing was going to happen and there was no stopping it.

Tomorrow morning the quiet farm country around my home would be the location of the release of fifteen hundred tons of nuclear inferno, even if we don't see it. I only hoped the portal would close before the detonation of all thirty of those weapons took place.

Chapter Eleven

BLITKRIEG

We had less than twenty hours to zero hour. I was sitting in a chair on the back porch listening to the silence of the evening. It was five o'clock and the sun was moving down toward the distant mountains causing the trees around the house to cast long dark shadows across the driveway and parking area between the house and State Route 191.

Just then Nancy came out the door onto the porch, walked over and sat down beside me. She looked out across to the field and said nothing for several minutes. "Todd?"

I looked over at her. "Yes."

"What's going to happen tomorrow?"

I sat there looking across the road, but

not looking at anything in particular, "I don't know."

She shifted in her seat, "Do you think we'll live through it all?"

I could hear a break in her voice and looked over at her. There were tears running down her face. "Nancy, I don't know what is going to happen once they launch their strike against the other Todd's dimension. I guess just about anything could happen.

"We were faced with one of two events happening in the morning. Either we were successful in the attack we had planned or we fail in our attack and they launch their own attack and our world would be fighting for its life."

She turned and looked at me. "Do you think they're doing the right thing?"

I felt myself take a deep breath. "Nancy, I don't think I even know what the right thing is at this time. I understand the terrible thing about to happen and I have seen the look in the eyes of all those people and know they wish they were someplace else other than here.

"My mind sees the necessity, but my heart feels the pain and terror about to befall those over there on the other side." By now I had turned in my chair and facing her closer to face on.

I reached out and put my right hand on top of her left hand. "Are we wrong? I don't know. But it does not mean we aren't right. I don't know and really cannot condemn nor oppose anyone over what is taking place. The other Todd lied to me and was deceptive in almost everything he said and did.

"Then he brought the other Nancy in and she violated my home. There is something terribly wrong there and I have this deep down feeling we need to protect ourselves. Whether the way we are doing it is right or wrong, that is my problem and I don't have the answer." I turned and leaned back in my chair.

She sat quiet for several minutes. I looked over at her and saw her hand was shaking slightly. I put my hand back onto hers and she looked at me. "Todd, have you thought much about death?"

The question cut into me. It was unexpected and took me several seconds to start my answer to her. By the sound of her voice, I knew she needed me to say something, so I told it like I felt it, "Nancy, to answer your question, yes. I have thought about death. I think it's perfectly normal for one to think of death and when, where, and how one would die. I look at death as a normal part of living. That may sound funny but after all my life has been a series of experiences, some good and some not so good.

"People seem to look at death as a finality, when, from my perspective, it's not a finality. I'm not just talking about the process of death, I'm talking about that yes, but I'm also talking about what comes after. I am certain death is not the end, but just a new beginning. What it is and where it is, I have no idea, but it is and I accept that.

"This then brings up the issue of God. Is there a God and do I believe in God? Well, to give you a short answer, yes, I believe there is a God. I can't prove it, nor will I try. Just accept the fact I do believe He is. When I look out at the world, I see such a marvel of mystery and beauty. The way it all functions and remains coordinated tells me there something there than just mere luck or happenstance. No, there is a God and I hope one day to meet him.

"Now, the issue of heaven and hell, well I feel when we die our living essence, call it soul or spirit, does depart this body. I have no idea as to how the good is separate from the bad, but I feel certain it is. We have heard of heaven and had been give many descriptions of it but I have a feeling anything we describe about heaven is nowhere near what heaven is actually like. As a result, I don't speculate about what it is and I target getting there instead.

"All right, that takes care of this issue, but what about the process of dying? Well, I feel it is as important as being born. It is the completion of my life here in this place. Just as I experienced my birth, even if I don't remember it, I will and must experience death. That to me is the exciting thing about death, it's a new experience, one I fully expect to witness and watch it happen.

"Don't get me wrong, I don't want to die, at least, not yet. But when the time comes, I want to witness it and take part in it. Do I have fears? Of course, I do. Everyone fears the process they may go through in their time of death. I hope and pray my time is painless and fairly quick, but I realize I have no control over how I die and when I die, so I try to be prepared for that one last worldly experience I will have.

"Do you understand what I'm saying?"

She sat there looking out across the road and field. Calmness had come over her and she was running what I had said through her mind. She looked back at me. "Yes, I think I do understand. I had never looked at it from that perspective. It was always a dreadful thing sitting out there waiting for me at some time and some place.

"And, yes, I have been fearful of it. It has always been an unknown, a thing out there stalking me and would, in time, find me and take me. I hadn't looked at it as part of life and another experience I would pass through. Thanks, it helps a lot."

For some reason I found it had helped me as well. Right now, we were facing a real threat to our lives and our way of life and there was considerable fear involved as well.

In addition, I realized each of us, every person there and involved in this project had a personal stake in all that was going on here. Each one would be thinking about the same thing Nancy and I had just talked about. Each one would deal with this event in their own way, some seeking another to help them understand and move ahead, and some dealing with it from within.

It opened my eyes to all the humanity working around my farmhouse that week. Each one doing what they had to do and still dealing with the possibility when it started it would not simply be a massive strike at the other side, but could progress into an all-out battle where all lives were at stake and possibly would be forfeited.

It's a sobering fact everything we know and understand could simply come to an end within the next few hours. I only had one last desire and that was to get to stand in front of the other Todd and tell him what I thought of him.

I wanted to hear his side of the issue and try to determine if his actions were just the cold direct actions of a committed individual hell bent on invading and taking control of another world, another dimension, and all those living within it. I found it hard to believe I could be that type of person. Yet, there it was and shortly I would know the truth and gain a new understanding as to Gods nature and His creation.

As darkness slid across the face of the farmland, I noticed a number of personnel exchanging position in their guard duties. The sky was clear with no clouds visible on the horizon. The stars came out in their full glory and it caused me to sit there and look off into space. How many other worlds were out there with people or maybe other living life forms? Were we fighting this battle for them as well, or was the same assault taking place on those worlds right now at the same time?

That sent a chill down my back. What if these beings from the other dimension were also invading some other planet at this same time? What would it mean to us? Would they in time get around to attacking us from space if they were successful on some other world? Gees, the idea of that caught my breath and it was possible.

I needed to set this all aside. There's no way we can even begin to know if it was true. The Nazi Party had never worked on space exploration, so the probability of that happening seemed to be almost beyond reason. Just the thought of it caused me to get up and walk out to the road and look across at the field where all hell would break out in the morning. I turned and walked back toward the house when Nancy came down off the porch and walked up to me. She put her head on my chest and I wrapped my arms around her and we stood there holding each other.

After several minutes we returned to the house and made dinner and sat down at the table. Neither one of us was hungry but we also knew we needed to eat something, if for no other reason than to keep from getting sick.

After dinner it was coming up nine o'clock and so Nancy decided she wanted to go to bed. She reached out and took my hand and then reached up and kissed me on the cheek. She said goodnight and started up the stairs. I turned and noted the Commander and his second in command were sitting at the table going over last-minute details.

I walked over to them and they recognized my approach. The Commander turned to me. "How you doing Mr. Hancock, how goes it?"

I kind of gave him a half wave. "It goes as well as can be expected sir."

He stood up and walked around the table to me. "Todd, is there anything I can do for you?"

I guess the look on my face probably told him more than anything I could have said. I stood there looking off out the window for a few seconds and then turned to him. "Yes, sir there is one thing you can do for me."

That night I slept poorly. It must have been around one in the morning when I heard the soft tap on my bedroom door. I got up and walked over and opened the door a crack and she was standing there. I opened it enough for her to slip in and then closed the door. She walked up to me and laid her head on my chest and we stood there.

After several minutes she looked up at me. "I'm sorry, but I couldn't sleep and I didn't what to be alone. I hope it's all right that I came here?"

I put my arms around her and whispered, "Its fine, I didn't want to be alone either."

She put her arms around me and pulled me close up against her and seemed to melt into me. She had the side of her face against my chest. "Can I stay with you?"

I run my hand around her waist and turned and walked her over to my bed.

It was a bright morning when the sun hit my bedroom window. I slipped out of bed and gathered my things and went into the bathroom. I finished getting dressed and cleaned up and walked out of the bathroom. She was sitting up in the bed with the blankets resting in her lap. "Good morning, Todd, thank you for taking me in with you last night. I didn't know if you would want me interfering with whatever you may have been doing."

I stopped and walked over to the bed and sat down on it. I took her hand. "Thank you for knowing I cared that much for you and being given the chance to show you. Never ever would you be interfering in anything I would be doing; it was something I needed just as much as you did."

She smiled and reached up and ran her hand along my cheek. "Funny how things seem to always work themselves out isn't it?"

I smiled, "Yes, I guess it was meant this way. Well, I'll go down and start breakfast. I think we will need to eat a good solid meal right now so we can deal with what is coming today."

She leaned over and gave me a kiss. I almost decided to postpone breakfast for another hour or so but got control of myself and told her to get up and I would see her downstairs. As I got up to leave, she smiled at me, "How about tonight?"

I looked down on her. "That would be fine and I was hoping you would say so."

As I entered the kitchen Duane was already there making the coffee. "Hi Todd, well today's the big day, how you doing?"

"Hi Duane, I'm doing just fine. A little nervous, but doing fine. What's the schedule for today anyway?"

He looked over at me, "Well, by ten the strike team will be in position and ready to take action. You and Nancy will be out of here and over around Lebanon in a safe place."

That stopped me, "Wait one minute. I'm not leaving my home when this thing is going down. I don't know about Nancy, but this is my place and I'm staying."

Duane looked at me and smiled, "You know I could have you removed, forcefully, don't you?"

By this time, I was standing toe to toe with him, "Yes, you could, but I would be coming back as soon as your people walked away from me. Look, I've been involved in this thing longer than you have and I think I have earned the right to be here when it all goes down. It's not that I want to be here, I feel I need to be here if for no other reason than to see this thing all the way through. Besides I already covered this with the

Commander last night and he agreed and set up a place on the back porch for me.

"As we talked, we both determined the other Todd will be looking for me when he comes through the portal and if I'm on my porch then that will give them the assurance all is well and their plan is on its way."

"And that goes for me as well. I've put a lot of myself into this project and I expect to be here through the whole thing." She was standing in the doorway to the kitchen looking straight at Duane.

Duane stood there looking back and forth between the two of us and shrugged his shoulders. "All right, you can stay, but you cannot get involved. Once things start moving you have to stay put and not say or do anything. The last thing these people need is some unnecessary surprise popping up behind them or whatever. Got me?"

I looked over at Nancy and reached out and took her hand. I was more than a little happy she wanted to be with me and that would set the stage for what was coming.

We both nodded our heads and I went over and started breakfast. As I was working on that Nancy said. "Duane, have you ever considered the probability there is another you over there on the other side?"

"Ah crap." I hadn't thought about that and it was obvious. What the heck was wrong with me anyway? I looked at Duane. "She's right you know. There is another you over there and he is probably as deeply involved in this thing on their side as you are here. What do you think of that?"

Duane leaned against the counter, looked at the wall on the other side of the room. "It's a most interesting idea. You're probably right, but what difference does that make. In fact, there is probably another of everyone here on the other side in the same positions or in other positions that bring them in close relationship to what they do on this side. But it still changes nothing. The bottom line is they could be there and they may not be there. It changes nothing."

The rest of the morning went uneventful for us. The strike team was busy as all get out as were their backup units and monitoring units. At seven thirty the strike team moved across 191 and moved into their blinds and prepared for the coming action, Nancy and I took up seats on the back porch. The Commander had set the porch up with the two chairs and positioned them in the best possible place in relationship to the location where the other Todd would be coming through.

It came to us as the other Todd and Nancy came through, they could probably see the house, and if they saw the two of us, they may not feel the presence of anyone else. Yes, we were important to this action, in fact we were the bait for the whole thing.

I expected the machine to come through at or near eleven o'clock that forenoon and as the time approached, I could feel the strain building in myself. I could see Nancy was becoming more and more agitated. I reached over and took hold of her hand and she seemed to calm down at that point. "I hate the waiting game. I have never been able to deal well with waiting. All I want is to get on with it and get it over with. What do you think, should I be out here so they can see me or should I go inside?"

I thought for a moment. "No, you stay here. I think they need to know there is someone else here who is involved and I have a feeling it would make little or no difference to them one way or the other."

Just then quietness seemed to come over everything. I looked at my watch and said, "Their coming. They should be showing up any second now."

I no sooner got that out of my mouth, when I saw the area over where the machine has always landed start to shimmer and move. I called out to Duane, "They're here and they're coming through right now."

Duane pressed his mic button. "All units, target is coming through at this time. Set up and follow the plan of action starting right now."

He no sooner said that when the portal opened. It was a round area that appeared like a bubble, light blue in color. The blue started to clear and as it became fully transparent the machine started coming into sight. At that point there was a clear line of sight through the portal and into the other dimension.

I heard Duane call out, "Fire."

Almost as soon as he said that I heard a loud bang and then saw three vapor trails come into view right out of the ground heading toward the portal. I felt Nancy take a fast-deep breath and then realized I was doing the same thing. All three rockets hit the portal at the same time.

The greatest concern of everyone involved in this attack was the issue of penetration of the portal. The question was, would the rockets penetrate the portal and enter the other dimension or would they simply bounce off. We had no idea what would happen. If they bounced, then we could kiss our days over and wait until it happened. If they passed through, we needed the portal to close before they reached altitude and went off.

As that thought came to an end the rockets got to the portal and passed right through. All three were perfect shots and just as dramatic was the fact as they passed through the portal closed. We did it. Damned if the plan didn't work to perfection. I could see the attack team wilting in their blinds knowing they did it and they would probably live through this.

The machine had landed in the exact spot it had been landing in and then all hell broke loose. I saw the rounds hitting the machine before I heard them. The one's that hit the front and rear of the machine hit almost exactly at the same time. I would hate to have my life on the line and depend on the accuracy of those rounds hitting their marks, but they were right on. The other Todd and Nancy had to have been scared near to death.

These were fifty caliber rounds and when they hit at that close a range they literally exploded. The hood and trunk lid both popped off the machine and she sat there and bounced.

Shortly after the first two rounds hit the third round hit the rear door and blew the door on the other side right off of the machine. With that I saw a cloud of red and white coming out of the door. It suddenly hit me there had been someone in the back-seat area of the machine. I hadn't expected that. Whoever it was, he or she was dead, sure as hell.

Just as fast, I saw the assault troops hit the machine. They punched the driver's side window and passenger's window out and jammed their weapons through the openings and into the machine. The doors came open and the front area occupants were jerked out of the machine and thrown to the ground. The whole thing took less than fifteen seconds and it was dead silent again.

Just then Duane came running out the door and across the driveway and across 191 to the machine. Right behind him was a number of other people, all carrying cases and other types of equipment.

A few minutes later Duane and his enforcement unit came back across 191 to the farmhouse with the other Todd and Nancy in cuffs. I looked at Duane and he was white as a sheet. I got up and met him at the top of the steps. "Duane, what's wrong?" Nancy was right behind me.

He stopped and looked at the two of us, "That round that went through the back door of the machine."

"Yes?"

He stood there looking at me, "It hit a man in the back of the machine, and killed him out right."

He started to turn and look back at the machine, "It was me."

I heard Nancy say, "Oh no!"

I reached out and put my hand on his shoulder, "Duane is there anything you need or I can do for you?"

You could see the shock setting in as he was trying to deal with what he had just seen. Just imagine walking up to anywhere, anyplace and looking down and seeing you laying there all shot to hell. This he had done and he was not expecting it. It was the furthest thing from his mind.

He knew there was another Duane on

the other side and probably fairly close in relationship to the other Todd and Nancy. But he had not guessed the other Duane would be there with them. He was physically sick and mentally numbed.

Finally, he looked at me, "I'm all right. It was one hell of a jolt, but I'm all right. Right now, we need to talk to these other two. Would you two, like to join us?"

As we walked into the dining room area, both the other Todd and Nancy were sitting at the table. The other Todd had his hands on the table top and sure enough he was wearing his SS ring. I looked at it and then at him and he sat back, looked at the ring and smiled at me. "You were more alert than I gave you credit for. I would have never thought you would have gone this far."

I looked at him, "Todd, what did you expect. You lied to me continually and the things you said and things you did were not matching up. I had to do something, especially when we saw through the portal and saw all the tanks sitting in the ready."

He sat there looking at the table top. "Yes, I can see what you are saying. I guess I underestimated you. I see you got your Nancy into the game as well?"

I looked over at Nancy and she was standing there looking intently at the other, the Nazi Nancy.

"Nancy?"

She looked at me, "Do I look that hard? I mean as hard as she looks?"

I didn't have an answer for her. "Nancy, I like you just the way you look. Don't worry about her right now. Are you ready for this?"

She took one more glance at the other Nancy, Nazi Nancy, and then turned to me. "Yes, I'm ready, so let's get this thing going."

Just then the other Todd spoke up. "We are prisoners of war and we claim our Geneva Convention rights."

Duane stepped up to the table and leaned over it, "Mister, the Geneva Convention does not apply to you in any way. Your government is not a signatory of that treaty right and therefore it does not apply to you."

The other Todd shrugged, "Well I guess we have an impasse then don't we."

"No, there is no impasse. You came here with one purpose in mind, the invasion of this dimension and as a result you are the aggressor and you will be treated as such. No Geneva, no prisoner rights, no access to your government. Mister, you're in what we call a no man's land. There is no one here who will stand with you and no one who will advocate for you.

Finally, I looked at Duane, "May I ask him a question?"

"Sure, go ahead."

I then turned my attention to both the other Todd and Nancy. "Do you two know what has happened here?'

The other Todd shrugged his shoulders. "What do you mean?"

I looked at the ceiling and then back at him. He was in a defensive mode and was not thinking. "Look, you may not have seen it when you came through the portal, but as your portal came into view a strike force shot three missiles each armed with a fifty megaton nuclear war head through that portal and into your dimension. Those missiles climbed to an altitude of fifteen hundred feet and then detonated. Do you know what that means?"

The other Todd sat there letting what I had said run through his mind and then a vacant look came into his eyes. "I don't believe you."

I turned to the computer at the end of

the table and brought up the video of the action that took place. He sat there watching as the missiles came into view and then passed over the top of their machine and passed through the portal. As they passed through the portal, he stood up slowly. Then the portal flashed shut and he sat back down. His face was ash white.

He looked over at the other Nancy and she in turn looked at him. She nodded her head. "Yes, that is what I saw as we came through. They were missile trails and they passed right over the top of us.

I leaned over the table toward him, "I don't know if those missiles actually went off, but they were designed to detonate when they hit fifteen hundred feet. Being in the military, you know what that means. It means one hundred and fifty megatons of nuclear energy were released over your tank force and whatever else was in the area at the time they went off."

I stopped to let what I had said sink in and then continued, "That Todd is our concept of Blitzkrieg. Do you understand now?"

Just then Duane stepped in. He laid the rest of the situation out for them. "Look you two. That was not all of it. We had reports of others from your dimension landing in several other locations across this country and the world. They were all met with the same level of nuclear assault when they came through this time. That means we had identified a total of ten portal location and we hit each and everyone with three nuclear weapons.

"Think about it, that's fifteen hundred megatons of nuclear conflagration hitting those bases in less than thirty seconds. That is what has taken place here in the last hour. Do you understand?"

It was then when Nazi Nancy broke down and they scooped her up and took her out of the room. The other Todd watched and finally took a deep breath and looked at Duane. "You sir can go to hell. I am loyal to my Fuhrer and you can get nothing from me, nor will I cooperate in anyway."

Duane then walked toward the kitchen and Nancy and I followed. When we got into the kitchen Duane turned to us. "I think we hit a nerve there. If I were to guess, we have dealt them a serious blow with our Blitzkrieg move."

I looked back toward the other Todd. "What now? What are you going to do with these two and the others if you were lucky enough to capture other invaders as well?"

He stood there a minute. "We'll continue to interrogate them until we are sure we have everything we can get out of them and then they will be eliminated."

Nancy asked, "Eliminated?"

Duane looked right at her. "Nancy, there is no place for them here. Also, we have no idea whether they are carrying anything dangerous on them such as germs that are from their dimension. No, they will be taken someplace and killed and then cremated."

Nancy quickly looked at me and then back to Duane. "You can't do that. They are living human beings and they have been convicted of nothing. You simply cannot do that."

Duane walked over to her. "Nancy, we have no choice. That is a United Nations Determination and direct orders. It has nothing to do with my feelings or desires. It's what has been ordered and that's what will be done. I have kept the two of you informed on this thing because you deserved the consideration, but at this point it has nothing to do with your personal desires. It is the cold hard fact and it will be done. This I can assure you, it will be done in a humane and painless manner, but it will be done."

Just then his phone rang. He answered it and stood there listening for several minutes and then acknowledged and hung up. He turned to us. "Well, that was the command and they advised one of the captured in Mexico has cooperated with them. They were able to use their machine and got a look at the other dimension. It's a waste land in all areas where we struck, total and utter destruction. They are sending a video to us so we can show the other Todd and Nancy and then maybe they will cooperate.

I looked out the window back across the 191 at the machine. I saw them loading a body bag into the back of a canopy truck along with a bundle of papers and hauling it away. A tow truck was backing into the field to take the machine away. In a few hours there would be nothing left of the actions that had taken place on this day. A battle fought between dimensions with the winner taking it all and leaving nothing in return.

I don't know how I feel. Maybe in a few hours or days I'll have a better understanding of my feelings and thoughts about this whole thing, we'll see. All I can say is it had to be done, there was no choice.

The other part of this thing was the fact we now knew we could be invaded from other alien worlds whether they were dimensions or planets. We were not alone and we were also a target. It made the whole idea of being a part of a bigger more involved cosmos much more intriguing and hazardous. We had a lot to do and a lot to learn over the next few weeks, months, and years. Yes, we were not alone and I feel sure in time we will surely wish we were.

I started down the back steps when Nancy came up beside me and started walking with me. I walked around to the opposite side of the house away from the 191 and then out into the field. I kept walking not saying a word with Nancy at my side also saying nothing.

We walked up on top of a rise I had visited all my life. It gave me a view out across the Kansas country side where all the dreams I lived, all those many years, had been dreamed and grown. It was my favorite place, my dream place and where I had planned my entire life in that spot.

It was past noon and there was a soft breeze blowing across the land and up and over the knoll. It had a smell to it that carried everything related to farms and the harvest and plowing of new fields. There were birds flying here and there and it all seemed surreal. Yet, it was so natural, as it should be all the time.

I turned and looked down on the farm house and watched as the last of the forces headed off down 191 back toward Lebanon. I felt Nancy place her head against my arm and take a tighter grip on my arm with her right hand and holding tighter to my right hand with her left. Nothing was said, there was nothing to be said.

The greatest battle the world had ever known just took place here in this small part of Kansas just six hundred feet from the marker for the center of the lower forty-eight states. As big as the battle had been the actual forces involved were small compared to all the military might available around this world.

This small force had taken on a battle-hardened military from another dimension and beat them back. Yet, now we knew we were not alone and in not being alone the hazards we were facing no longer rested solely within this world or this dimension. It now ranged through the entirety of the universe and the realm of the dimensions.

If God had meant to design his creation this way, then he really worked overtime. With the realization there were other forces out there that could and would try to take us under their control was a sobering realization. That caused me to wonder what God was thinking when he created mankind or life for that matter.

I guess it's outside my ability to grasp and understand. All I know is right now, here in this one single spot where I would sit and think through most of my life and dreamed of the future, I found the future I had dreamed of was nowhere near what was actually happening.

Fifteen weeks ago, something had happened that changed everything for me and for that matter every human being on the face of this Earth. It turned out to be a nightmare and has caused the death of an unknown number of people in the other dimension. The question is should I have had any feeling toward the other side?

The answer is yes, I must have feelings because if I don't then we as a civilization have a hopeless future ahead of us. The fact is within that other dimension there were people who had no part in the actual plan for invading my world. They were like so many others who live day to day in this world and think nothing of what the military or governments of the world are thinking and doing.

How many of those civilians paid a price for their government's actions I didn't know. It was hoped there would be none, but I knew the truth and it told me a lot of innocents died over on the other side and I should be aware of that and have some sense of feeling toward them.

Chapter Twelve

BACK TO THE OTHER SIDE

Everyone was up at the usual time and had a good breakfast that morning. It was six hundred hours and they had two hours to the launch of the machine back over to the other dimension, Dimension Fifty-three. Todd and Nancy were sitting with Duane discussing their actions once they landed on the other side. As with everyone else just before a strike force was launched, they were nervous.

Duane advised them the nine other sites were on schedule to launch their Blitzkrieg at the same time. Over all there would be more than two million personnel committed to this invasion. It was the usual process of hitting them fast and hard. If all went as planned it would be all over in three to four months.

Nancy found herself feeling a sense of pride and accomplishment. "I just know we will achieve everything we set our sights on. However, I do find myself worrying about the other Nancy over there. I do hope she will be all right."

Duane sat back and looked directly at her, "Nancy that is not your concern. The other Nancy means nothing to us. She is one of them and whether she lives or not means nothing, nothing at all."

It sounded brutal, but she knew he was right and all the worry in the world would not make things better for anyone, even those over there. This was what they were there for. Nothing in the entire universe was more important than bringing new life and the Third Reich to these dimensions. It was their salvation and our purpose.

They decided to walk over to the launch site that morning. The weather was perfect and they needed the time on their feet. Once they were in the machine it would be a considerable amount of time before they would be able to get out and move around again. Besides, it gave them the time to finish preparing for the jump.

She looked out around the area and focused on the Concordia Mountains off in the distance. It was a gorgeous day in Kansas. The sky was clear and the temperature was a perfect seventy-two degrees. They could not have asked for any more perfect weather at the jump off time.

Todd looked around at the level of activity going on around them. Every manner of preparation was taking place. Men were checking their guns and other equipment they carried into battle. Tankers were making sure all their onboard systems were working and they had a full load of fuel and ammo.

The lead tank was at the portal position, its squadron flag up and waving in the breeze. As he looked across the field of tanks, he could see each squadron flag up and waving. Each squadron had a different color for its battle flag and each tank in the squadron had those battle colors on their turret in the shape of a swastika.

Each squadron had a fleet of support vehicles that would fall in behind them as they passed through the portal. There were fuel tankers, ammo carriers, rations and field hospital carriers and so on. Wherever the tanks went, they went.

Attached to each tank squadron was a battalion of ground troops. Their job was to do the clean up as the tanks moved through an area. These troops were to be transported by troop carriers immediately behind every fifth tank through the portal. Each carrier had a maximum of thirty troopers on board and each unit of troops could carry out an assault on any hard point they came against. All in all, it was a most efficient organization and process.

The three of them continued across the base to the launch sight. When they got there the machine was all ready for its jump. Nancy got in the front right, the co-pilots position, and started to set up her programs and tracking system. Colonel Miller got in the back seat behind Nancy and belted up. He had the main command radio in his position.

Todd checked the machine out and then entered the pilot's position and completed his pre-launch check list. They had fifteen minutes to launch and everything appeared to be in prime condition. He was prepared to land and then exit the machine and go immediately to the other Todd and take him into custody. It was vital he carried that action out and complete it in less than five minutes.

If he were lucky the other Todd would be coming to meet him.

Once the other Todd was in custody then Nancy and Colonel Miller would exit the machine and move over to the farmhouse and set up their command base. The next unit through the portal would be the rest of the command and operations center personnel and hardware. Right behind them would be the first of the tank units.

If all went well, they would have seen a full squadron of tanks and their support through the portal within the first two hours. At that point the second and third incoming portals would be on line and a steady stream of tank squadrons would be passing through.

Finally, Todd's launch radio came to life and the launch commander checked in with them. "Scout Unit, are you ready?"

Todd pulled his seat belt tighter and replied, "Scout to launch, we are ten by ten."

There was a pause and then, "Launch Commander to Scout. Launch countdown starts right now."

Todd reached over and pushed the power switch and all the interior lighting came on. He then replied, "All systems up and functioning."

Launch Commander continued, "Six, five, four, three, two, one, all systems activated and launch initiated."

There was a flash of gold light igniting all around the machine and they felt the machine lurch into action. The portal came to life and a bubble appeared around them and they felt the machine lift up and start to float. It felt like it was going nowhere, just sitting there or hovering. After what seemed like an hour the gold color faded away and the bubble turned to a blue color and they felt the machine lurch. That was the passage into the other dimension.

Just then Nancy called out and pointed. "Look, what's that?"

Todd looked to his left and saw three white lines of vapor coming at the machine. At the same time Colonel Miller called out, "We have incoming hostile fire."

The objects passed over the top of their machine and right through the portal and then the portal snapped shut. Almost at the same time the machine was hit by two rounds, one in the front and one in the back. Both rounds blew the hood and trunk lid off the machine.

A third round slammed into the back area of the cockpit where Colonel Miller was sitting. They heard him grunt and then felt the round slam into the right rear door and that door shot off its hinges. Todd looked back at the Colonel and saw he had been hit. The round almost blew him in half. He had died instantly.

Todd hit the intercommunication button and advised base they were under fire. Base came back with a garbled message and then Todd heard what sounded like a loud rumble and explosion. At that point the base went dead.

Next thing he knew he was being pulled out of the machine and thrown to the ground and cuffed. It was a trap, but how did they know. He could not remember any time in the past when this had happened, none whatsoever. They were laying for them and those rounds passing through the portal had to be nuclear, they had to be. Shit, the whole invasion had been destroyed and they didn't get a shot off.

Meanwhile, back at the jump off point the tank squadron commander was in his tank preparing for their jump into Dimension Fifty-three. He was watching the scout machine start its jump and saw the portal opening. Just then he saw three white streaks come through the portal directly at him. It was so close he ducked as they passed over head. He turned and watched them curve upward and head straight up.

It would be the last thing he ever saw, as the rockets reached the fifteen-hundred-foot mark, they all three detonated. One Hundred and fifty megatons of nuclear weaponry went off at once. The flash from the detonation literally burned the eyes out of everyone looking at it. In fact, the incident was so new, their experience with it was zero, and everyone who was in a position to look did just that.

Next came the shock wave and it was followed by the heat wave. The two combined to literally melt anything and everything within a fifteen to twenty-mile radius. At the same time the same action was taking place at nine other points where their military was making their jump into Dimension Fifty-three to carry out their invasion.

That was a combined total of fifteen hundred megatons of nuclear conflagration hitting their army at one time in each of the ten locations. The damage was far more extensive than just the military units being hit. Their attitude was so corrupted they felt no one could withstand their forces in a full-blown invasion. They were so confident of their actions they had jump off points in the middle of huge metropolitan areas. Areas with populations ranging from ten million to well over fifty million people.

Through the captured scout machines the leaders of the Dimension Fifty-three defense forces were able to view the Father Land of the attacking forces and see the extent of the damage. It was devastating. General estimates of damage ranged from severe to catastrophic or total annihilation.

There was nothing observable that gave them any indication of the percentage of survival. Nothing that found any surviving forces capable of launching a follow up attack at that time. All that was left was to develop some means of preventing their attempt at launching another invasion of Dimension Fifty-three, and that would follow within days. From the Dimension Fifty-three military's stand point they had figured a way and were sure they would be able to block any attack in the near future or ever for that matter.

Further out from the detonation areas the leaders of the Third Reich, who were watching the launch of the attack, witnessed the counterattack and then the nuclear detonations. They tried to run for cover, but they were still too close to the ground zero explosions. They were literally fried where they stood and none escaped. No one knows what fifteen hundred megatons of nuclear explosions would do to a world. It made little difference at that time, it would take hundreds of years, if not thousands, to recover if ever.

The rest of the citizenry of that dimension knew something really bad had happened, but none would be able to grasp the magnitude of it. How can a multi-million-man invasion army be destroyed to the last man in just a matter of seconds? So fast not a single round of ammunition was fired in the launching of the invasion, all of it to the last rounds, the last vehicle, the last person was gone.

What they saw as just another invasion and just another dimension that would fall to their armies has turned out to be a disaster. It took days before they started to fully understand what had happened and by then it was too late. Too late to prepare for the following spread of the radiation that had been released. Too late to deal with the loss of their ability to produce, their ability to cultivate, harvest, process and distribute, that which was needed by the general public to survive.

A population who had never experienced defeat in any way was now facing the worst of the worst that could befall them. They were now realizing their battle had just begun and it would rage on for years to come.

With the spread of the radiation and the dust produced from a fifteen hundred megaton conflagration, their world would be driven into a nuclear winter. They would be hit with radiation poisoning, failure of agricultural crops, and the loss of the heat and energy of their sun to provide the much-needed environment they had to have to live. The loss of life would be extensive. In a way those who died from the aftermath of the detonation of fifteen megatons of nuclear bombs face a more horrible death than those who died instantly.

The trauma to the social order would bring about a blow to their civilization and the organized and ordered society they were accustomed to. In one short burst of time all had changed and it would take years upon years to recover. They were entering a time of civil disobedience, civil war and social death. They had been knocked back two thousand years and would probably never see the glory they had enjoyed again.

Only the survival of the fittest would reign as the rule of power and survival during these times. Only cunning and determination would be rewarded with survival and success. To the pampered it was hell in all its ramifications and the hardest of reality.

A society of beings who were accustom to receiving and taking orders was now on their own. It was a lost society, one that had no direction, or understanding of what happened or was coming and no ability to deal with it.

The fragmentation of this society would reach fully around the planet, touching every single individual. The die off would be horrendous. What would be left would be pockets of organized peoples fighting to survive against all the odds they were faced with. That would turn into direct group on group combat with only one side of the combat surviving.

Government would come back and would attempt to regain control, but that would take time and time would involve many years to overcome all that resulted from the destruction of their military capabilities.

Yet, there were other concerns and those had to do with food supplies and the rebuilding of their ability to reproduce that food supply. Then there were the results of the radiation effect on new births across the world. What would that do to those coming behind, those being born into this new environment. Only time would tell.

Chapter Thirteen

LIFE GOES ON

Meanwhile, back in Dimension Fifty-three, things had calmed down and most of the security forces who had been living and working around my farmhouse over the last five to ten days had left the area. The machine was gone and the field cleaned up and it looked like nothing had ever been there.

All of our paperwork, tapes and videos had been taken and we were left with nothing to provide us with any evidence that a major event had taken place at the center of the lower forty-eight states. Nancy and I had returned from the field back of the house and stood at the driveway entrance and watched the last of the forces leave the area. As the last vehicle pulled on to 191 and headed east, Nancy walked over to me and took my hand. "Feels kind of empty, doesn't it?"

I held her hand in mine, "Yes, almost like nothing had ever happened at all. That is, except for you. You are going to stay a while?"

"Well, as long as you want me to."

I squeezed her hand. "Let's work into this and then plan for the long haul in a few weeks. What do you say about that?"

"Todd Hancock, are you proposing to me?"

I felt my face flush and stood there looking off across the 191 at the battle site. "Well, it's only been a couple of weeks that we have been together, and I did not want to jump the gun, but I was hoping."

"Yes, I will." She said as she squeezed my hand and cuddled closer to me.

We went back into the house and looked over everything we had left. "They left little of nothing behind. Todd, I'm sure glad we have the safety deposit box full; it should work into a great book."

I was nodding my head as I looked around the place. "That's exactly what I was thinking. We are going to make a great team."

We still did not know, nor were we given any idea as to whether the bombs went off and if they did what had happened. We knew there had been considerable damage as a result of the dimension machine down in Mexico being used to view the other side. But that was only one area and did not take into consideration the totality of their war machine.

It could well be our side didn't know, or they knew, but were not letting anyone know what the results had been. We made it our goal to find out what the actual results were and to see if the danger from the other dimension was still a concern or not.

Two days later a car pulled into the driveway and a single man got out, it was Duane. We met him at the door and let him in. As he entered, he was looking around and then said, "You two making a nest here?"

Nancy laughed, "Yes Duane, we're making a nest."

He looked at us. "Good, I could see you two were meant for each other. I really hope all goes well for you. Oh, please invite me to the party, all right?"

We nodded at him. "Duane, what are you here for? Did you forget something?"

He turned and looked over at our computers. "Well, I guess I came by to see if there was anything else, we failed to find and remove. Do you have anything related to the event here?"

Nancy walked over to the desk and picked up an envelope. "I found this upstairs in your room. I was going to mail it to you, but now that your here, you can take it with you."

He took the envelope and opened it. Inside were the notes of several of the meetings he had made during the planning phase of the event, as they were calling it now. His eye brows went up and he looked at us, "These only copies of these papers?"

"Yes. I had considered making copies, but thought better of it. They're not mine and I don't want any trouble from your group."

I then walked over to him. "How about you staying for lunch and then we can sit back and reminisce about the past couple of weeks, that all right with you?

"Yeah. I would like to do that. Mind you though, I can't tell you a lot. Everything about the event is now classified and I can say little about it."

We ate and then moved out onto the

porch with our coffee and sat down and relaxed. Duane was the first to speak. "Todd, what was your take on the way this whole thing went down? I mean, were we fair or did we take undue advantage of you?"

What a question. I had not thought about it before. "At first, I thought you people moved in too fast. That was my initial reaction to everything. But, as I thought about the situation and all that had to be done, it was really reasonable overall.

"I don't remember one person being disrespectful. In fact, several of them bent over backward to accommodate Nancy and me. The tactical team commander was most helpful and clearly understood the strain and difficulties we were experiencing. I was grateful for his presence. The rest of the team was just as respectful."

Nancy leaned forward. "Duane, I have never been as scared as I was as I watched this whole event go down. I kept asking myself if there had been a better way to handle this whole thing. But, I too, came to realize this was way beyond anyone who was here, the commander, his troops, you, and us. The situation ruled and we had to live with it and within it. I don't want to use the term brutal, but as it turned out, it was and it was also necessary."

Duane was listening intently. I could see the concern in his eyes as he sat there letting us get anything and everything off our chests. He took a deep breath and leaned forward. "I guess I need to let you know the end result of this event.

"We were able to get the machine to operate again. We discovered it had a communications capability between it and the other dimension. Once we got it working, we were able to get a look at the other dimension location. As we looked, we saw the level of destruction that had taken place. I can tell you it was not anything I wanted to see.

There was row after row of destroyed tanks over there. We were able to get a view of the area off and away from the primary assault units and everything was down and fire damaged. I would say it was probably ninety percent destruction."

I didn't what to hear that. "Duane, what about the other Todd and Nancy, what is going to be done with them?"

He smiled and sat back, "Well, it was decided not to terminate them. They are still being held in a secure location and will probably spend the rest of their lives there. The other Todd is holding his ground, but Nazi Nancy, along with most of the others, has started to talk and give us information about the overall plans of the invasion.

"As it turned out we were one in a long list of dimensions they had invaded and taken over. It was their goal to overrun every other dimension they could find and gain access to. She explained not all other dimensions are accessible. They left them for later on when they had developed other means of achieving access.

"Probably the most interesting thing we have learned was how the Nazi Party gained control in their dimension. It happened as we had figured it had. Hitler and the others had been able to develop a machine capable of giving them access to a dimension, any dimension. When they jumped, they had no idea where they were going and what they would find.

"As it turned out, they landed right in the middle of a society with was many generations behind them in their development. Basically, they were seen as gods and this is how they gained control so fast. When they got things moving the people simply fell in line. The rest you already knew."

I then asked him. "What is the potential then, of other societies, coming against us again in the future?"

"That Todd we do not know. We know a huge part of their military capabilities were totally destroyed in our strike. But we do not know what their industrial capabilities are. Right now, Nazi Nancy is not willing to talk about anything we want to address. I am sure in time she will and then we'll have a better idea as to what to expect. Our best guess is we knocked them back a few hundred years or so. At least I hope so." Duane replied.

"However, we have determined, through our questioning of some of the other scout units if we make the landing zones they came in at completely unusable, then it will probably end their attempts. So, it has been decided to build block houses at the sights and stop any further use of those locations.

"That does not mean they are permanently stopped, but it will mean they will have to start over from scratch and then rebuild everything. As we understand it, that is a huge undertaking and one costing more money than you and I could even imagine. No, at this point they will weigh the cost against the need and it will probably end there.

"So tomorrow, around noon, a construction team will pull up across the road from your place. They will build a huge monolith made up of reinforced concrete. This thing will be so big and so heavy nothing, not even a direct hit by a nuclear weapon will move it. Sorry kids, but you will have a solid mass of concrete one hundred by one hundred feet and buried fifty feet into the ground and reaching fifty feet above the ground sitting across the road from you."

He sat there waiting for our response. All I could do was breathe out a heavy "Great."

Nancy was a little more animated. "You have got to be kidding us. Something like that sitting out there only a hundred feet or so from us is not acceptable. I will not stand for it."

Duane sat there a few moments and then raised both hands. "Sorry kids, I have no say in this. All I can tell you is what they told me and it is coming no matter how angry you get or are. So, I would suggest you get used to it and think about some way to take advantage of it, whatever it may be."

After a couple of hours Duane stood up and walked to the edge of the porch and turned. "Well, I guess I have to leave. Don't forget to invite me to the party when you two take the plunge."

He started down the steps and when he got to the bottom he stopped again and turned, "Oh, by the way, I realize you probably have a lot of data holed away on this event and I can understand that. However, you need to know if you write, record, broadcast, or in any way communicate information to anyone else other than between yourselves, it will be a violation of federal law and you will be subject to prosecution.

I just thought I should let you know that those words came right out of the mouth of the Attorney General himself, and I would further tell you he means it. Got me?"

That my friend is called Checkmate but it was not the end of the game. Knowing Nancy as I do, she'll come up with something that should just about seal our fate. Hopefully they would house us in the same location as husband and wife.

My job was to try and be tempering in the process and mitigate her desire to jump out of the pot and into the fire. It should be one interesting game. However, I had one extra ace in the hole, once married I was fairly sure she wanted a baby and, well, you know a mother's instinct. She would never put her child in danger of seeing its parents taken away, yes, that would work.

Oh, the monolith across the road? She talked to the contractor and they agree to paint it whatever color she wanted and then plant some trees along the road between us and it. I was impressed with the way she got them to cooperate.

Each day she would walk over to the sight and stand there and watch. After a few days of thinking she started getting up earlier and making a batch of cookies or some other treat and started taking them over to the crews at the morning and afternoon break times.

In short order they were expecting her and soon after they were giving her sole and total access to the area. When she got to that point, she started asking questions and making suggestions. She got her paint job and the trees. It was all cordial and mutually achievable for both sides.

So, today we have a monster of a monolith sitting across the road. On the side facing our farmhouse is a painting of the landscape behind the monolith and a line of trees running along Country Road 191 finishes the effect and the monolith all but disappears from sight.

That same process was incorporated at the other nine sights as well and everyone came out ahead. My only problem is, when the monolith needs to be repainted, is that going to be my job or will she manage to get the government to come back and do it again. I hope to hell she gets their cooperation.

Now all we had to deal with would be the line of conspiracy seekers hitting our door every day of the week. We knew it would be coming. Things like this simply do not go up without someone asking questions and then you have a limited amount of information about the battle that took place here getting out and that is enough to get the conspiracy game going in high gear.

As we thought about the issue Nancy started to smile. I knew almost immediately she was scheming again and something was coming at me, if it did not get me put in jail, could well get me ducking for cover.

"Conspiracy stories sold like mad and if we actually masked our story in that kind of a scenario, we could probably get our story out there and then leave it to time and providence to bring the rest of the truth out into the open."

Good grief, she was actually thinking about a book. That was going to get us into so much trouble I thought we would have to abandon our home and head someplace where they did not have extradition treaties with the U.S.A. Yet she was right, something needed to be said about what took place here on that day.

A lot of people took part in this action and the hazards were off the chart for them and this nation. No, the country deserved to know about it and this would be the way to do it. As I think about it, no jury would even so much as consider finding us guilty.

Yet, we still had to think about those on the other side. Not knowing how and what they were doing made it that much harder. It was impossible for us to think a society would be so committed to its government it would readily support the invasion and colonization of other dimensions, but that appears to be exactly what had happened.

The Nazi's from the invading dimension had done just that. They found a place where the population was well behind them in its development, then they brought in their socialization and technological superiority, and in no time, they had the whole of that dimension, or should we say that world, that other Earth, accepting their concepts and social structure to the person. It made the Germany of 1930 look like child's play.

I guess the politically minded being is universal across all the cosmos. All they need is a group of people who will listen to them and accept what they say as the truth. Usually, within a group of people there are those who don't believe what is being said, or they resist the activity they are witnessing.

In that case, those who resist or disagree are simply removed. During Hitlers time it was called the Night of the Long Knives. A time when Hitler's brown shirts moved on all those across Germany who opposed the Nazi political stand.

It happens in every totalitarian government; a time comes when a cleansing of all who appose or resist the new order are singled out and removed. In Communist China it was during their Cultural Revolution in which the youth or young followers of Moe carried out a cleansing of China's society all based on Moe's Little Red Book or Quotes.

In Russia the Bolsa Vicks carried out a cleansing of the elite and all political parties opposed to Communism. The object being to remove any resistance so their totalitarian system could take full control of the country.

Now the world has had its primary government destroyed and with it came every conceivable political idea there are minds thinking about it. They're a long way from being what they were before this event. First there would be the forming of groups and then the move to dominate other minor groups and then major confrontations for total control

No, they had a long way to go and a long time to get there.

Chapter Fourteen

REMNANTS

After a total of thirty nuclear bombs had gone off across the face of their fatherland, there was not much left to look at or to collect and use. In effect, a nuclear winter set in and the majority of those who were not killed in the initial blast started to die off due to the radiation effects across the face of their world.

Plants, animals and especially people started to die off in mass. There was a mad rush by the government to try and save as many as possible, but even with all the technology they had, the loss of life was monumental.

Priorities were given to those who were

high up in the Nazi party, or were scientists or masters of industry. The masses were left to fend for themselves and their die out was stunning. Across their world bands of people formed up and started developing centers of power and then they started to encroach on the territories of other groups. It was a case of the survival of the fittest. Small but fearful battles sprung up across the land, and in time, some groups vanished, while others grew in size and power.

Many of the surviving bands would group together, knowing their odds of surviving improved when they combined their skills and resources. That resulted in fewer organized bodies or groups, but their ability to defend and attack improved as well.

The central government and those it targeted to save grew as well and they then pushed their knowledge and power of industry into the forefront in the battle for control of their world. Many massive battles were fought between the government and those groups who had won out over others and then challenged the government itself, the battles were ruthless and merciless.

When the government was challenged, they killed everyone and every living thing.

Whole areas were wiped clean of life. It was an all or nothing situation for the government forces and they hit without mercy and took no prisoners.

In time the government was able to produce the machines of war they needed in such numbers only it could produce. Then it set out to regain control of the whole of their world. Even at that the number of people gathered together was only a fraction of the great warring world it had been before. There was no give or take in these battles. There was one simple rule, those who killed more of the other side won, and to ensure the other side never came back, the kill was one hundred percent.

Though they were coming back, the greatest loss to their ability to wage war was the loss of the technology that had been the foundation of their war machine. Nothing survived, except for a few notes and samples here and there. Nothing to write home about, but maybe enough to bring them back to the time when they jumped from dimension to dimension, spreading their ways and concepts of life. Would they be able to achieve that level of advancement again? Only time would tell, but the comeback was under way and there was now nothing to stop them.

One thing that was burned deep into their minds was, never to return to Dimension Fifty-three. No matter what they were going to achieve or how well they did it, Dimension Fifty-three was off limits. Well, at least for now. Maybe a hundred years from now they would take a shot at it, and maybe they would let a bad memory lie.

Anyway, nothing of that time and the technology that took them there survived the nuclear holocaust that warm summer day, those many years ago. A proud and well-trained army met its match and they were reduced to but a remnant of what they had been. Where millions and billions once lived now it could be counted in the hundreds of thousands and a big army of any kind cannot come from a resource that small.

Yes, in time their population would rebound, but they had other concerns to deal with. It was still unknown what the infusion of all the radiation would do to the people or to the animals of their world. In time they would learn and then deal with it.

Finally, after years of strife and hardship, the government of the Nazi party returned to ground zero of the ten jump off points. By this time vegetation had over grown most of the area and the presence of radiation was still at a level considered unhealthy.

Still, they managed to erect huge monoliths of reinforced concrete at the location of each jump off point. Partly to block any future attempts by the Dimension Fifty-three governments to invade their land. The other reason was to give recognition to all those who had lost their lives in the attempt to invade and overcome Dimension Fifty-three.

Each monolith was one hundred by one hundred feet in size and was buried fifty feet into the ground and stood fifty feet above the ground. They were sure no one or no machine would be able to back track them and enter their domain. It was the right and smart thing to do, and it gave a sense of safety to those who were still present.

The great grandnephew of Todd Hancock felt sure this was the right thing to do, as did Nancy Paulson's family descendants. They all stood there looking at the monument as the final paint job of the landscape around the area was completed and trees were planted along the country road they were standing by.

Their struggle was just beginning to start and just how they would fare would not be known for hundreds of years. No, they would no longer be a threat to any other dimension. And, by the time they could be, their desire or social will to do it may well have died as well.

The remnant of the Nazi world had spawned a return to its old glory and it had taken root and was expanding. What was evident there was no longer the will to expand beyond this place, their world. So, the gods of war had thrown the dice and they had lost. They were no longer seen in a favored way and so, they abandoned history and settled on a new and less deadly future.

What they failed to see or understand was they had created a number of other Nazi worlds, and they were far more dangerous than they had ever thought possible. Payback was about to settle on their land.

Finally, the time of Adolph Hitler was over. He started a war in another dimension a hundred or so years ago and when beaten down there, he came to this dimension and rebuilt his dream. It grew and spread across the dimensions until it ran head long into Dimension Fifty-three. At last, the Blitzkrieg of the great German army had been blunted and stopped dead in its tracks.

Was this the end of the Nazi war machine as we knew it? In the world Hitler and his cohorts ended up in it was. The only problem is they had been building this mind set into their people for years and the other dimensions during that time and those dimensions were still of that mentality. Hitler may be gone but the remnants of the Nazi Blitzkrieg still remained and as long as it was there, it was a danger to any and all dimensions. There were fifty other dimensions they had attacked who were of the same mindset, and the possibility of them striking again increased with each dimension was still of the Nazi system.

Chapter Fifteen

ONLY TIME WILL TELL

Three weeks after the monolith had been completed and the world had settled down and the usual state of affairs was back to normal Nancy and I sat at the kitchen table looking at all the paperwork we had on the event.

We had the disks and recordings and all the paper work we had developed during our investigation of the dimensional event that had taken us so close to death and the loss of all we knew. This was the legacy of that event.

We had finally set a date for our wedding and Nancy was settling into life at the farm. Our purpose now was to start a book that would be created as a fictional story of a great invasion of the United States from a quiet location in the northwestern region of the State of Kansas. It was just six hundred feet from the marker for the center of the forty-eight contiguous states and was dwarfed by the presence of a concrete monolith sitting across from our simple farmhouse.

It was important we stayed with the fiction plan with anything that would even so much as resemble an attempt to brand the book as being based on factual events would bring more trouble down on us than we would ever want to deal with.

Yet, we wanted to base it on an attitude of fact and build it as a fictional story. We wanted to gain access with the other Todd and hoped we could make the move and still keep from violating the mandate set down by Duane on his last visit.

Why did we want to talk to the other Todd? He held the answer to several questions that were haunting us and we felt we needed to know the answers before we could continue. It had more to do with his life's story and how he came to live in Wichita instead of the Lebanon area. We were looking for the building of another character for the book, but we wanted it based on factual elements and not just speculation.

We had contacted Duane and invited him to our home to talk to him about the book and what we wanted to do. It was a gamble, but one we thought would be beneficial to both of us, that is the government and us. The idea being, if we could develop a relationship with the other Todd and Nancy, then maybe they would open up and provide the information we needed and what the government wanted as well.

Somewhere off in Texas a number of people from the invasion force were being held in tight security and being put through extensive questioning and interrogation. Slowly but surely, they gained the information they wanted and needed in regards to the political and social makeup of the other dimension.

Along with the social and political goals the scientists gained more information on the operational capabilities of the dimensional jump machine the other dimension had used. We had already obtained extensive technological benefits on the radio systems and telemetry system in the machines. The next thing they were after was the navigational technology they had developed.

S.S. Captain Todd Hancock was standing firm in his refusal to cooperate with the officials at the facility where he was being held. But still, they would not give up on him. He was the only one of the prisoners who had the most information and knowledge locked up in his head. If they could break him, they could make technological leaps of tens of hundreds of years. The goal was the key to space and dimensional travel and they wanted it badly.

The other Nancy had been cooperating with the government all along. She was trying to gain as much of a relationship as she possibly could and hopefully end up living in a place that was more to her liking. Basically, she wanted to get out of the prison environment and into a more public residential environment. With that goal in mind, she held nothing back and had even tried to get the other Todd to cooperate. That turned out bad and almost cost her, her life.

Why all this maneuvering anyway? The battle was over. One side won and one side lost. It was our fortune to come out on top and as the victor we were trying to collect its winnings. The other Todd did not agree and would not agree.

Whatever the case, there was a lot of bargaining taking place with little gain resulting. We were of the opinion if we had a shot at the other Todd and or Nancy, we could come up with the information everyone was working so hard to obtain. Was that a guarantee? No, but there was a good chance of success from our perspective.

It was shortly after noon when Duane pulled into the driveway. We quickly dumped all the disks and paperwork into the box and placed them in the closet. We met him at the back door and let him in.

After the greetings we invited him into the living room and settled down to talk with him about our plan. When he heard about the book he immediately went on the defense. "You two know you're stepping into an area you have been told to stay out of?"

"Duane, we are not writing a factual book. We are writing a fictional story about a fictional attempt to invade this world from another dimension. That is completely different from a biography or any factual subject matter. We feel we are on strong ground on this and wish to pursue it.

"However, it is not why we have asked you to come here. We want to meet with Captain Hancock and the other Nancy and talk to them about their time as children and how they ended up living where they said they lived. We are trying to put together a story of two men from different dimensions who meet in unusual circumstances and end up on the opposite sides of the fight."

Duane sat there listening to our argument and then replied. "I don't know about that Todd, Nancy. It sounds too close to the actual event and it could well be seen as a rather poorly cloaked attempt to tell the actual story of the battle of Lebanon as it became known."

Finally, I leaned toward Duane. "Look Duane, this is a story I find most appealing. Everything we write and say about the event will be based on fictional locations and actions. We live right here. We don't need half the world showing up at our door step trying to discover something no one else knows.

"I am most curious about the comparisons between our respective lives and how we eventually came to meet as we did. That is all we are trying to do. In fact, we are prepared to let you or anyone else preview our book to insure we do not release anything seen as secrets concerning the events that happened here.

"We are looking at changes in time, place and people involved. The primary characters will be the two men from the two dimensions as they first meet and as the events change their lives take change in response to what is happening. Yes, we will use the actual event as the basis of our story plan, but this foundation will be the extent with any relationship to the actual location and event."

Duane sat there looking at the two of us. "You're not trying to circumvent the secrecy directives on this event?"

"No Duane, Nancy and I are simply trying to write a book. This thing has been eating at us for all this time and we need some way of getting it out of our system." By now I was leaning almost across the table toward Duane. "I don't know about you but every minute of that happening has left a scar on our souls and we have to have a way of releasing it. We can't tell the true story, but we can tell a stylized version of the story and do it in such a way so there is no connection between the reality of what happened and the story in our book."

We all three sat there looking at the table top when Nancy reached over and took my hand. "Look Duane, I saw the reaction you had to seeing your counterparts' body that day. The look on your face was something I was grateful of never having to experience.

"I know it still haunts you because the whole of the event still haunts me. Duane, I need to do this, it's important to me. It's not a money game or anything else. It's a release of time and the memories that will not clear my mind. We all need this. It is something so important there are not enough words that can be said to get it across to those who never experienced it."

Thirty minutes later Duane was walking out to his car as Nancy and I accompanied him. When we got to the car he turned. "You two know I'm placing a lot of trust in you. If you do this wrong or if you have lied to me it's going to be devastating for the three of us. They will hit you; they will take the three of us out, and it's will leave no record of our involvement with the government or anything in the area of my home. There will be no place any of us can go to get away from them. This thing is locked down and is to never be made public, no matter how important it was.

"I don't agree with the plan, but I'm not the one in charge, the politicians are. They have talked among themselves, across the whole of the world and they mean what they say. Hell, they had a number of them who wanted to simply kill you both and probably me as well. You have got to understand this must be so separated from the real event you are willing to put your lives on the line for it."

I knew he was right and our very lives would be on the line if and when we wrote the book. Still, I pushed the point. "Duane, Nancy and I know what you're saying and we agree with you. Let me say this, there was a time when we looked at this event from a career point of view. We saved the files and planned an exposé in the future. However, between the original time and now our attitude and needs have changed and that is no longer the case. Now it's for our own welfare and nothing more. Do you understand?"

He stood there looking at the ground and then looked at the two of us and smiled. "Yeah Todd, I do, and that's why I agreed to this project. I will work with you two in every aspect of this book and I want my name attached. I think I need this as much as you two. I just want us to realize there is a tight rope here and it's not four lanes wide."

Duane got in the car and looked up at the two of us. "I'll call you on the date to see Captain Todd and the other Nancy. Until then just hang tight it may take a few weeks to work it through the system."

It was more like four months before Duane called back. He had a date for us and it was a tight schedule. We had three days to get down to Texas and they were giving us just two days to talk to the other Todd on the condition the other Todd wanted to talk to us. After meeting the other Todd, we would get four days with the other Nancy.

Four days later we were sitting at a table in a small room at the facility where they were holding the other Todd. Because of his attitude and resistance to any and all questioning, he was being held in this one location all by himself. They had separated him from those he knew and from the rest of this dimension. He was living in total isolation and under 24-hour guard. There was a force of over four hundred personnel manning this one small base to insure he remained here and he did not have the opportunity to kill himself as well.

As he entered the room I stood up and looked directly at him. He stood there a few seconds and then moved over to the chair on the opposite side of the table and sat down. Not a word had been said. We sat there looking at one another, and then he did something totally unexpected, he reached out and offered his hand to me to shake. I did the same and we both sat back and he then spoke.

The other Todd seemed to be a little uncomfortable in the meeting situation, but he placed his arms on the table top. "First of all, I wish to tell you I am sorry I violated your trust in our relationship as I was scouting this dimension. I feel with all that has happened you are the one really innocent one here and it was wrong for me to treat you in that manner."

I sat there looking at him. I felt my mouth drop open because this was totally unexpected on my part. Then I had a sudden feeling of doubt and suspicion as to why he would apologize to me. What was he up to?

Finally, I got my voice. "Todd, I don't understand why you are now making this apology. It does not seem right nor does it seem sincere. I'm sorry if this hurts your feelings, but you caught me off guard and now I find I have sincere concerns for what you may be up to."

He sat there looking at me and nodding his head. He repositioned himself. "Look I will never apologize for doing my duty to my nation and my government. But I feel I can and should apologize for my individual treatment of you. You need to know in our plans for you and Nancy here were to ultimately be executed as a means of getting you out of our way. For that and the rest of my attitude and action I am truly sorry."

That was a revelation neither Nancy nor I had expected. I had to sit there and think over all that had happened for a few seconds, and while I was doing that he said. "Todd, it would not have been me doing the execution. We have rules of conduct that exempts us from killing ourselves in other dimensions.

"They are there because of the psychological trauma which can result from an act like that. Yet, I was still there and I knew of the plan and had agreed to it at the time. I have rethought my action and I regret them."

A quiet fell over the room and all three

of us sat there, not looking at anything in particular nor thinking much about anything. The other Todd finally broke the silence. "May I ask what your reason is for being here at this time?"

That brought my attention back to our purpose and I address our plan. "Todd, Nancy and I are writers. Our careers go back a number of years and as a result we have determined we want to write a book about this event. Now it will not be a factual book but a fictional book playing on our two characters.

"In a nutshell we want to tell the story from a perspective of our two separate lives, you in your dimension and mine in this dimension and then the interaction as we met the first time.

"Why we want to do this is twofold. First and foremost, we need an outlet for our emotions as a result of the event. We need some outlet that will help us get over it. Second, we felt it would make a great story people would want to read and experience. We are not looking to write a factual account of what happened, they, the government, will not let us do that."

He sat there looking at me and Nancy and finally sat forward. "How can I help you in this endeavor, that is, if I agree to assist you?"

"Todd, you can help by telling us your life story. How you got to that particular career and how your youth was. What schools did you attend? What were your favorite games as a youth? What your home life was like? How you got along with your parents? Generally, we are looking for things about you growing up."

A smile moved across his face and he asked. "You don't want to know about our technology and war machines? You're not interested in our training and social development under the Nazi style of government and its expansion across our dimension?"

That caused me to smile back. "No, were not interested in any of that stuff or the history of your military and the actions of your governmental systems history. We want something more personal, we want your story, the story of your life as you grew and as you became involved in the Dimension Fifty-three event and nothing more."

Finally, he nodded. "All right I'll work with you, but I want to have the option of stopping whenever I determine it is in my best interest."

With that I looked at Nancy and we both nodded our agreement. "This is how we want to progress. Nancy will act as the moderator and will ask the two of us specific questions about our lives, and then we are to write them down so we can compare the two lives over the years from our birth to the present. Is that all right with you?"

He sat there a moment. "Interesting, I think I would enjoy this process a lot. Would I be able to see your answers as well?"

"By all means, I want you to see them. I think it would be just as interesting to you as it would to me." I was leaning back again and looking at Nancy for her response as well.

She was nodding her head. "You will get a copy of everything we cover and how you both answered."

With that Nancy handed out a note book to both of us and several pencils. She moved to the head of the table and the two of us sat facing one another across the table.

The questions started. Nancy would ask a question and we would write our answers and then tear the page off the notebook and hand them to Nancy and she would stack them beside her one on top the other. This went on for a day and a half and the stack of paper beside her grew to several inches high. There must have been five hundred pages in the stack when she finally got to the end of the questions and we handed our books and pencils over to her. She got up and left the room while the other Todd and I sat there and talked. It was then he got even more personal.

He suddenly said. "You know Todd I had a young woman back home who had accepted my proposal of marriage, did you know that?"

That hit me hard. "No, I didn't know. Did she live in Wichita?"

"Yes, she did. We were to be married at the end of the Dimension Fifty-three invasion and I was so looking forward to that day. I'm sure she died in the counter attack. At least I hope she did. That would save her having to face the aftermath of something like this."

I could feel his hurt. "I understand Todd. Nancy and I are getting married shortly and I can't even imagine losing her, especially that way."

We fell quiet again and shortly Nancy returned to the room with two stacks of paper and placed one down in front of the other Todd. He looked at it and then at us. "Will you two be coming back again in the future?"

Nancy smiled at him and leaned over. "You better damn well bet we will be." I nodded my approval.

We stood up and walked over to the door. Todd sat there watching us and I had a hurt feeling come over me. He was doing his duty and now he was a man without a nation, a world or a dimension. He had to be the loneliest man in existence.

Two days later we arrived at the holding facility for the other Nancy. As we entered the interview room, she was sitting there in exactly the same outfit my Nancy was wearing. She stood as we entered the room.

The two Nancy's stood looking at one another. Finally, my Nancy stepped forward and reached out with her right hand to shake the other Nancy's hand. She responded and the two of them stood there holding one another's hand. After several second, they both embraced.

I stepped forward and shook the other Nancy's hand and then we all sat down. I let myself settle into the background and let my Nancy start the conversation. "Nancy, Todd and I are here because we need to meet and talk with you about what has happened. We are not here to represent our government we are here for our own welfare. Are you willing to talk to us?"

She sat there looking at both of us. "I have been questioned by more people than I care to talk about. I've told everyone who had come here everything I know, there just is nothing else to tell."

My Nancy started to shake her head. "No, this is not what we want. Nancy, we want to talk about you and me and what our childhoods were like and the things we liked and did. We want to know you and I especially want you to know me. I can't tell you exactly why I feel this way I just do."

She was nodding her head. "Yeah, I know what you're saying. It would help me too. I'm so lonely for home and I just don't know where I'm going or what they're going to do to me. I'm all alone and it's killing me."

My Nancy was clearly shaken by what the other Nancy had just said. I noticed a tear run down her cheek. "I have no idea as to what it is like to be in your situation. But I can see it is something I would hate to have happen to me. Nancy, I don't know where you and I will be going from here, but if we can help each other then I'm willing to work with you."

The other Nancy was looking at my Nancy and then she put her head down on the table and started to cry. Her whole body was shaking as she let it all out. My Nancy got up and moved over by the other Nancy and put her arms around her shoulders. The other Nancy then moved around and put her head on my Nancy's shoulder.

After about ten minutes my Nancy moved back over by me and we sat there waiting for the other Nancy to compose herself. Finally, she said. "I will work with you on your project, but I have one other thing I want to ask of you."

My Nancy then asked. "What is that?"

"I want to have an ongoing relationship with you. Would it be possible to continue writing letters and maybe some phone calls in the near future?"

My Nancy sat there. "I would love to have a relationship with you, I think it would be good for both of us. I will even go as far as to say if they ever decided to let you out of this place and you need a sponsor to leave here, I will be the sponsor for you."

That caught the other Nancy by surprise. She sat there shaking her head. "You would do that for me after all that has happened and if we had taken you captive, we would have killed you?"

"Yes, even with that. Nancy it's over and we, you and I, have the rest of our lives to live. You are no longer in your own dimension and in fact you are homeless. You need someone here and I'm willing and I believe Todd is willing too."

She smiled at the two of us and then sat back. "I would love that. Now what do you want of me?"

We laid out what we wanted to do. It was the same we had done with the other Todd. She agreed and we set things up with me being the moderator and the two of them sitting opposite each other and writing out their answers.

A day and a half later we finished the project and copies were made and one set was given to the other Nancy. The two of them exchanged addresses and my Nancy and I got up and bid the other Nancy good bye.

Two days after we got home Duane showed up to collect his copy of the interviews we had with the other Todd and the other Nancy. He was impressed with the level of detail we had collected and thanked us for the information. We all walked out of the house and to his car. We shook hands and he got in his car, closed the door and left.

I took Nancy's hand and started walking toward the 191. We crossed the road and walked over to the monolith and stood there looking at it. To the public it was a navigational marker for high-speed aircraft being developed by the military. We knew what it was and why it had been placed there.

We had lived through this time and had experienced something few across this world had ever experienced. It was a moment in time when the very existence of this world, as we knew it, was in danger of ending. Nancy had developed a close relationship with the other Nancy and they were permitted to call each other on a weekly basis, and their letters could be exchanged anytime they wanted.

It was a relationship I found odd but warming as well. In effect they were just like twin sisters and their relationship was growing each and every day. It would turn out fifteen months later they gave the other Nancy a closely monitored release to live wherever she desired. She moved to Lebanon, Kansas and started working as a receptionist for the local Doctors office. Just like sisters the two of them spend a lot of time together.

Todd? He's still held in the same facility and will probably spend the rest of his life there. I have been permitted to meet with him two other times. Those meetings have resulted in me being given the privilege to visit him on a monthly base a plan he fully agreed with.

In time the other Todd started to talk to me about the details of his career in the SS on the other side. He talked about the indoctrination of new recruits and what they went through as they developed and pledged their lives to the system.

As we talked and got to know each other in detail he started to loosen up knowing this was his life now and he would never go back to his home dimension. It was most interesting as we came to trust one another and recognize just how alike we were.

It was three months later when I arrived for our regularly scheduled visit. I was sitting in the meeting room, at the desk, when the door opened and in walked Todd. "Well, look at you. Don't you look different."

There he was walking toward me dressed in casual attire. After all this time he was not wearing his uniform and he looked great. "And what do I need to know that has happened over the last month?"

He smiled and sat down across from me. "Look different?"

"Yeah, you do. In fact, you look great. What brought this own?"

"Well, I got to thinking this past month and my holding out was doing nothing for my living conditions. No one challenged me about it, they simply let it be. It finally dawned on me this was my life, the way it has gone and I can do nothing about it, so it was time to live it. To live what I am and where I'm at."

"Yeah, I see what you mean. I'm proud of you. I don't expect you to embrace this dimension, but I think you could still have a life that would be rewarding to you. I don't know what the governments feel or think, but I'm willing to work with and for you to make your next step.

He smiled at me. "Look, I'm an SS Officer. That is written into my mind and I can't just dump it. I will always be one and that is it. I have to accept it and then deal with it. I have a long way to go before I could walk out into your world and take it as it stands.

"I have a long way to go before anyone

could even begin to trust me. You and I have come to know each other more intimately than I have ever know another person. But I still have the stigma of the SS from your worlds past history to deal with and from my own dimension as well. This is my first step. Not only do I have to prove myself to your government, but I have to prove myself to me. And, the most difficult of the two will be me. The reason was as I try to leave my military life behind me, my own inner self will be accusing me of being treasonous to my own dimension.

"That may sound odd to you, but for me, it will be a struggle I will have to fight for sometime and that is where you come in my friend. I will need these visits from you to help me in my struggle. I know I can make the change, but like anyone else I will need support.

"Yet, I was personally involved in a scheme that would have cost you your life and I find it difficult to try and draw you into this thing, but I still must ask."

He sat there looking at me. He was a strong man, but like anyone else, he needed support when facing the difficult. I was sitting there having seen the full activity and impact of that August day near my home. I was scared, but at the same time I had Nancy with me. The event, no matter how bad it was, was the one thing that gave her to me and I have never been more grateful.

I stood up and walked around the table to Todd's side and sat down in the chair next to him. I looked him straight in the eyes. "If you need me, I'm going to be here for you. I can't change the past; I can't make this thing better for you. But I can be here to help you take the steps you need and want to take."

He sat there and I saw a tear slip down his cheek. Without any other though we both reached out with our right hand and took hold of one another. "That, will save my life, thank you."

That was two years ago. How did Todd do in his plan. Well, he did well enough he was able to move out of the holding facility and set up a home in Kansas, actually about five miles from me. He has started to visit with Nancy, from their dimension, and things are starting to get interesting.

Will he keep moving ahead? I don't know, but right now he is doing well and if I have my people figured right, there will be another Todd and Nancy wedding in the not too far future.

Yes, I walk across the 191 every Monday of every week and take a long walk around the monolith. Was it for the remembrance of the events that took place there? In a way yes it was. In reality I come over weekly and checked for cracks.